BEST
FRIENDS
FOREVER

BOOKS BY SHANNON HOLLINGER

The Slumber Party

BEST FRIENDS FOREVER

SHANNON HOLLINGER

bookouture

Published by Bookouture in 2023

An imprint of Storyfire Ltd.
Carmelite House
50 Victoria Embankment
London EC4Y 0DZ

www.bookouture.com

ISBN: 978-1-80314-894-6
eBook ISBN: 978-1-80314-893-9

To my grandmother, Marvis, reader and adventurer extraordinaire, for teaching me that being strong, tough, stubborn, and bookish are excellent traits for a woman to have.

THE LETTER

The words leave me gasping for air. Folding the letter, I tuck it back into the envelope. Clutch it to my chest, against my pounding heart, as I push the chair back from the table and stand. My knees buckle, striking hard against the floor as my useless legs fold under me.

All these years, I believed my best friend was a killer. And then I came back home, and I dared to hope that she was innocent, only to have my mind changed again and again. But now I have the answer. Now I know for sure.

And yet I still feel absolutely devastated. It's too late to make it right. How will I ever live with myself?

By finding the person who killed Emma and making them pay. I need to find a way to hold myself together long enough to see this to the end. To get justice for Emma. The thought scares me. Because the way I feel about this person? It makes me want to give them a dose of their own medicine. The lethal kind...

PROLOGUE

Murmured sobs carry on the warm night breeze. Rumors whispered in low voices. Nervous glances move through the crowd like a virus, faces lit by the strobing red and blue lights.

Uniformed police officers mill about, trying to keep order. The detectives want to talk to everyone present, but it's impossible to keep track of who they've already spoken with, as the knotted clusters of students pulsate like a beating heart—but there's one heart among them that will never beat again.

It was only a short while ago that laughter filled the air, voices filled with enthusiasm and excitement. And why not? They were celebrating. It wasn't every day that they graduated.

If eyes grew glassy with too much drink and the imbibing of an illegal substance or two, well, that was forgivable. They were on a precipice. On one side awaited the rest of their lives as they stepped into adulthood. On the other, the childhood they were leaving behind.

Some had been friends their entire lives; others were enemies almost as long. But tonight none of that mattered. Some of them would never see each other again. Trespasses were forgotten, vendettas paused. Kisses were lingering and sloppy. Because they'd done it. They'd survived high school.

And among them, one girl, far younger than the rest. A girl who shouldn't have been there at all.

Her older sister holds her tight, refusing to let her go. Alternates between promising her that everything will be all right and answering the detective's questions, because the young girl? She cannot find her voice. Not after what she's seen.

They'd expected it would be a night to remember. It became a night they'd never forget, but wish they could. Murder has that effect sometimes.

ONE

"Hello?"

Holding the umbrella forward against the slanting rain, I tuck the phone between my chin and shoulder and continue searching my purse for my keys. Managing to hook my finger through the key ring, I curse as the wind catches the umbrella. I drop the keys and fight to keep my scant shelter from the storm.

A gush of breath on the other end of the line reminds me of the phone at my ear, of the caller who still hasn't spoken. I'm about to share my frustration with the pervert breathing in my ear when the wind strikes again, yanking my umbrella inside out, exposing me to the deluge of rain. I'm instantly drenched, but that's not what chills me.

Dropping the useless umbrella, I stare helplessly at my locked car. Somehow, I know who the caller is. My breath catches and the name comes out in a whisper. "Lily?"

A soft noise, like that of a fingernail scratching across the mouthpiece of a landline phone, carries twice through the line. I touch the driver's side window with my fingertips, like the wet glass is her damp cheek, trying to steady my nerves.

"Lily."

The noise comes again. It's her.

"Is everything okay?"

I wait, but the line remains silent.

"Can you put Mom on the phone?"

Nothing. It's like one of the games she used to love to play, where she'd make me guess the answer. Only this isn't fun for either of us.

"Lily." I swallow hard against the knot lodged in my throat. I don't want to say the words. I don't want to ask, because I already know the answer. She wouldn't be calling, otherwise. I feel tears mingle with the raindrops on my face, scorching hot against freezing cold. "Do you need me to come home?"

I see her hand in my mind, her pale, tapered finger nodding yes against the phone as I hear the noise.

"All right then. I'm coming. I'll be on the next flight out. I promise."

I hear the click on the other end of the line, feel it as a physical reaction inside my skull, and then I'm numb. That's when you know a cut is bad, when you watch the knife sink deep and nothing happens. The reaction is delayed, but you know what's to come. The dark blood welling from deep, slowly at first, then steadily, a faucet that has no switch. And then comes the pain. The pain is always the worst when at first you feel nothing.

I give myself a moment, waiting for the bleeding to start, waiting for the pain, but it doesn't come. This cut is too deep. When my body finally reacts, it's going to be devastating.

Picking the keys up from the ground, I fumble, dropping them again before I finally get the door unlocked. Sliding behind the wheel, I make no effort to spare the interior from my soaked clothes. There's no point. It doesn't matter now. Nothing does.

I've used up my reprieve. It was longer than I expected,

more than I deserved, but it's over. Now it's time to go home, to face what was started so long ago. I'm not foolish enough to believe that I'll ever see the current life I live again. Like a snake, I will shed this skin and leave it behind. Like a lamb, I will allow myself to be led to slaughter.

TWO

The rain stops by the time I find a spot and park on the street. The apartment is dark and empty. I've already stopped thinking about it as home. Maybe I was foolish for ever doing so.

My belongings are few. I pack what I'll need into a duffel bag and leave the rest behind for my roommates. Grabbing the bag of cat food from the kitchen, I step onto the narrow patio, the two-foot strip of crumbling pavers crowded with weeds that separate the apartment from the alley.

A head pokes out from between two rotted panels of wood, round amber eyes staring at me with anticipation. I crouch. The cat hisses, flattening its body against the fence, only to be shoved over by the fat-headed tabby with half a missing ear pushing through the gap. The tabby brushes against my knee, then swats me with an angry paw. Anxious mews, from the mouths of tough, weathered cats and kittens, fill my ears as they gather in the alley, crying for their free meal.

"Sorry, guys." I empty the bag of food onto the ground, spreading it as much as I can. "This is going to be the last time."

They eye me suspiciously, pacing, waiting for me to retreat from the pile of food, this representation of love and hate, need and fear, of symbiotic want that I've worked so carefully to cultivate. I stand and the furry bodies rush toward the kibble, all deep throated growls and sharp clawed threats as they share the fight for survival. This is the world I know, the one I lived in, the one I thought I'd escaped. This is what I'm returning to.

Locking the door behind me, I watch for a moment as a battle-scarred tom bats an emaciated looking scrap of fur over the head, claws curving into the scalp, holding the kitten away from the food as the stronger cat eats. I want to intervene. I want to make sure each belly gets its fill. Yesterday, I would have gone back outside. Today, I turn my back. My reality has changed. Now I have to focus my efforts on my own fitness to survive.

Scribbling a note on the back of a receipt, I leave it on the counter with my keys and the signed title to my car. My room-mates can sell it to cover my portion of the rent while they find someone to take my room. Grabbing my bag, I adjust the strap over my shoulder and take one last glance around. It feels like my last look at civilization before entering the wild.

I walk down the street to the MTBA, carried along by the momentum of the people around me, just like it's any other day. Scanning my card, I descend the stairs and find my last stroke of luck, the train I want just pulling into the station. I fight my way onto the blue line, like I'm going to work, but in my heart I know I'll never see that place again. This time I'll ride the train to the end.

I've never actually been to Logan Airport before. Or any airport, for that matter. I didn't come here, to Boston, directly. It was just another stop on a series of long, dusty bus rides north. I stayed because it was a city large enough to lose myself in, far enough away to create a new identity, and I could get all of that while still being near the Atlantic Ocean, the only thing from home that's still with me.

My fellow passengers mind their own business, eyes averted

as they're spit on and off, with lurches and starts, until only a few people are left as we pull into South Station. I follow those with luggage up the stairs, standing to the side of the group as they gather at the curb. I let them board first, then take a seat on the back of the Silver Line bus, feigning the experience I lack. When I left Florida, I barely had enough money to get me to the next county. Now, I can afford a ticket for my first plane trip.

I pretend to be a seasoned traveler as I enter through the glass doors of the airport, blinking against the florescent light and stale air. Joining the nearest line inching its way toward a counter, I hope I can fake my way as painlessly as possible through the experience. I perform each step in the process like a robot, detached and emotionless. It's almost like an out of body experience, like I'm watching myself from afar, because this behavior isn't a sign of who I am, but a symptom of what I've become, which is painfully numb. Shock courses through my veins, choppy and frozen like a slushy, and I've got a killer case of brain freeze.

I find myself strapped into a seat on a plane with little memory of how I've gotten here. Outside the window, I watch as luggage is loaded onto another aircraft. Suitcases full of memories stowed for safe keeping. I think of my own duffel bag, shoved into the dark belly of the plane, and wonder if the weight of the secrets I keep has rubbed off on it, weighing it as heavily as my limbs.

A man drops into the spot next to mine. My seat lurches with the force and my mind flashes to every news broadcast of a plane crash I've ever seen. I swallow the thought, pushing it down deep into my gut with the rest of my fear, and notice the man beside me staring at my white knuckled grip on the arm rests. I tear my hands free and tuck them under my thighs.

"Nervous flyer?" he asks.

He grins at me like he enjoys my discomfort. I tell myself

I'm imagining it and force myself to look at his thick, beefy face, skin the color of raw pork, and smile.

"I don't know. This is my first flight."

Something about my answer offends him. His lip curls as he glances at me sideways with disgust. I close my eyes and take a deep breath. Count to ten. Run through all the positives in my mind, all the things I have to be grateful for, all the qualities I possess that I should be proud of.

My level of anxiety tics down, like a car engine cooling off. When I open my eyes, I look at the person sitting on my other side. A grandmotherly woman lifts her head to give me a polite smile, then returns to the book she's reading.

It's been a long time since I've done that. Imagined hatred and disgust and horror aimed at me from every direction. Attributed feelings to strangers who don't yet know how they should feel about me. The plane hasn't even left the ground yet. I'm still over a thousand miles from Florida and it's already begun.

I close my eyes again and push my head back into the seat. There's no use lying to myself. The life I'd constructed, my little sliver of happiness and normalcy, is over. Just like that night ten years ago, things will never be the same again.

THREE

Unfurling my fists, I rub my sweaty palms across the thighs of my jeans to dry them. I stare out the taxi's window and focus on my breathing, trying not to think about how every rotation of the tires brings me closer to where I don't want to go, nearer to the tiny town with its narrow streets haunted by dark secrets and ugly memories that I've avoided for almost a decade. I swore to myself that I'd never go back. Yet here I am.

The cab jolts over a pothole and my eyes flash open. The palmettos lining the road blur together in a constant stream of green. Angry gray clouds hover overhead, threatening an afternoon thunderstorm. These are the colors of my childhood, of car trips and playing outside and looking out the window on rainy days. I shouldn't be here.

Veering right, we exit off the highway. My surroundings quickly become familiar. The movie theater where I had my first kiss. The grocery store where my mom would go to buy the good cookies. The elementary school where I played a donkey in a play. The streets are lined with memories that quickly become so painful that they leave me breathless. Pressure builds inside my chest, welling up into my throat like a scream begging for release.

I try telling myself that I'm only going to be here for a short time, just a quick in and out, but I know that's not true. I don't know what's happened yet, what twist of fate has occurred to bring me back to this place, but I do know one thing—now that it's gotten its claws back in me, there will be no escape. I won't get the chance to leave this place again.

Then I see her. Like a dog I push my nose to the glass, watching her walk down the street like she doesn't have a care in the world. Like she hasn't haunted my dreams, turned them into nightmares for so many years. Like the weight she carries on her back is so much less than the weight on my own.

Emma Daley. My best friend.

My worst enemy.

My... I don't know what.

But as the cab rounds a corner and she disappears from view, fury spills down my throat like a bitter medicine. Resentment that my mom and sister insisted on staying in the house, in this town, despite my repeated attempts to get them to move someplace else. Someplace clean and untarnished. The anger immediately morphs into remorse.

Of course my mom would want to stay in the house, the place where the memories of my father live. The place where Lily's voice used to sing out in waves of fairy-tale laughter. Endless happy babbling like a meadow brook bordered with wildflowers, only to be quenched, to dry up in a single instant, never to be heard again. A wave of queasiness unsettles my stomach and then I'm angry again, this time at myself.

The truth is, a part of me disgusts myself. A large part. I knew I was going to have to face this place again, eventually. I guess I was just kind of hoping for a longer respite. Not that ten years isn't a nice stretch, it's just that forty would have been better. But the day has come. There's really no way around it.

And I'm pissed at myself for being such a wimp. It's not who I am, not anymore. Except, maybe it is. Maybe I don't know myself as well as I thought.

Now here I am, refusing to get out of a taxi in my mom's driveway. I've paid the fare. Made some polite small talk, but I've run out of things to say and now it's gotten awkward. The cabbie's dark eyes are squinting at me in the rearview mirror. I think he's getting nervous. I know I need to get out of the car, but I can't.

Then the front door of the house opens. Panic flies up into my throat, choking me, my heart beating wildly as my mom's neighbor, Marilla Lynn, comes towards me, pulls me out of the cab and into a hug. The driver seizes the chance to be rid of me, gets out of the car and pulls my bag from the trunk before driving off without another word. I'm still being flopped around like a rag doll by Ms. Lynn, pushed and pulled as she inspects me from every angle. This must be what hell is like.

"Kate, honey, I can't believe it! Let me have a look at you. You look absolutely gorgeous! Yet, there's still no husband. How can that be, dear?"

"Hi, Ms. Lynn. How are you?"

"Oh, well, I creak a little more every day, but that's to be expected. I've nothing to complain about, not like your mother, bless her heart. How is she? Have you come to take care of her while she's on the mend?"

I look over her shoulder, my eyes drawn to another familiar face, this one lingering in the doorway. Lily. All grown up.

"Actually, Ms. Lynn, I'm not exactly sure what happened. I just know that there's been some kind of trouble, so I came."

Ms. Lynn glances behind her, where Lily slumps against the doorframe, arms crossed with the impatient angst only a teenager could muster. But she's not a teenager. The face I'm staring at is that of an adult. My baby sister is a woman. And a stranger.

"Oh, dear, I feel horrible, I should have thought to call you myself. Your mom had a slip in the shower. Nothing too serious, she's going to be fine, but she's broken her hip. Gonna be on the mend for a while. I wonder why she didn't call you? Must not have wanted you to worry. Of course, there's a rapist on the loose right now, so maybe that's it. Can you believe that? In Wakefield! I thought I'd never see the day..."

It surprises me, too. Wakefield had always felt so safe. At least it had until that night.

I watch Lily disappear into the house, the elusive Nessie slipping back into the waters of the Loch, and a wave of protectiveness washes over me. I smile at Ms. Lynn and nod, feeling the thin veneer of composure I've managed to fake slipping away. Grabbing my bag, I squeeze past her on the walk, saying, "It was great seeing you, Ms. Lynn."

"Oh, yes. I'm sure we'll get plenty of time to catch up now that you're back home. I can't wait to find out all the details about that job of yours and what's going on in your life. Your mother is so stingy with the details. Really. And I—"

"That sounds great, but right now I really have to run. I need to go check on my mom."

"Such a dear. You're quite right, I can't even imagine how uncomfortable your mother must be right now. The sheets they use on those hospital beds, so rough, it should be a crime. Seems like they should be able to use some nicer linens for what they charge nowadays..."

The door falls open as my hand turns the knob. I drag my pack inside and smile and wave as I shut the door on Ms. Lynn, locking it behind me in case she tries to follow me inside. My head buzzes from her rapid-fire chatter, but I'm pleased to discover that the panic has subsided in the wake of my escape.

And then it hits me.

I'm home. The place looks exactly the same as I remember it, and though I don't recall the house having a smell, the aroma of cinnamon and vanilla that wraps around me like my mom's arms can only be described as the scent of my childhood, like clean laundry and fresh-baked cookies. I get a little weak in the knees. I guess I hadn't realized that you could miss a place as much as the people who fill it.

Everything I look at charges my brain with memories of the happiness I experienced here, the love I felt, the life I lived within these walls. This place is a piece of my history, a piece of my soul, from the chair my dad used to sit in, to the mantelpiece over the fireplace that I pushed my cousin Parker into, chipping his tooth, to the coffee table in the living room where I banged my shin at least twice a week for years. This place fits me like a tailored glove.

But then why am I so uncomfortable?

I look around again, this time seeing everything as if from a great distance—the one that separates me from this old life. Maybe if I hold on to it hard enough, it'll keep me insulated, like a layer of blubber.

I leave my bag next to the front door, not ready to see my old room yet. Not willing to get settled. I wander into the kitchen and find the keys to my mom's minivan hanging in the same place where I used to covet them as a teenager.

I can't help but look over my shoulder as I lift them off the hook, like I'm doing something bad, and another memory strikes like a flash of lightning. I stole the keys and took the minivan that night. It's how we got out there, to that dense copse of pines and palmettos where I saw a waking nightmare that has haunted my dreams ever since.

I expect the familiar fingers of panic to return and give me a squeeze, but instead I feel nothing; I'm emotionless as my feet retrace the steps I took that night, leading me to the garage. The door creaks open. Flipping the switch, florescent lights spark to life overhead, humming loudly. One flickers like a candle flame in a draft. In the center of the room, a dull, navy behemoth waits beside my dad's classic Roadster, the one my mom started driving after his death. The trance is broken.

Lily sits in the passenger seat of the faded blue minivan that was already ancient ten years ago. She cocks her head sharply in my direction, chin lifted in a defiant manner, eyes slightly narrowed. Locking the door, I climb behind the wheel and look at my sister, my first good look.

Her blonde hair has darkened with age, more than mine. It's copper now, falling softly around her shoulders with a reddish glow. Her cheekbones are higher, finely chiseled in a face that's lost the roundness of youth. Her eyebrows are shaped into perfect tented arches, no longer the fuzzy caterpillars I used to tease her about.

Every time I blink her image is momentarily replaced by the face I remember. Young. Chubby cherub cheeks. Eyes full of curiosity and hope. I shake my head, clearing the slate of my mind like an Etch A Sketch and redraw Lily in my memory as she is now. A beautiful grown woman.

Suddenly, it's too much. The numbness that's blanketed me in my shock melts. A sob escapes my throat as I throw my arms around her. She stiffens in my embrace. It breaks my heart, and, with it, the dam that's held back my tears.

"I'm sorry, Lil, so sorry. I never should have left."

Her body softens against mine. She smells like cherries and rainbows and sunshine. She smells like my little sister.

"I was just so scared, and I felt so bad, so guilty, and I ran. I was a coward. But I'm going to do whatever it takes to make things right. I promise."

She pulls back. Her eyes dart around my face, as if searching every pore for a sign of treason.

"Do you think you'll ever be able to forgive me?"

Her held tilts to the right, her face softening. She nods.

"Your eyebrows are fantastic."

For the first time in years I see my sister smile, revealing perfect, white teeth.

"Wow, your orthodontist must have been a miracle worker."

Lily hits my arm, her face scrunching in mock anger, but her eyes still smile.

"Is Mom at Mercy General?"

She nods.

"Should we go try and break her out?"

Another nod, and once again I'm struck by how beautiful my baby sister has grown. I feel a sharp pain in the pit of my stomach, clawing fingers of acid spreading up my chest, into my throat. I swallow hard, forcing the guilt and bile back down.

The real challenge, the thing I know I'll never quite be able to do, is to forgive myself. I'm the one who robbed my sister of what had promised to be a bright future, as sure as I'm the one who robbed her of her voice, her normal childhood, her inno-cence. And for that, there is no absolution.

FOUR

Kate glances over her shoulder to make sure that they're not being followed, the darkness pressing in around them as she pulls Lily through the woods. They have to go farther, move faster. They have to get away.

If they can.

Because every time she closes her eyes, she sees it. The horror of it has sunk under her skin, is spreading like blood through her veins. Like poison. And if what they saw is having that effect on her, what's it doing to her baby sister?

It's her fault that they're out here. Her fault that her sister saw...

"We can't tell, Lily. Not Mom, not anyone."

She swats at a mosquito on her neck. The insect's body sticks to her sweat-soaked skin. Its innards streak her hand. Seeing the dark smear on her palm makes her shudder.

It's amazing how much blood can fit into such a tiny container. The contents of a body under such pressure, just waiting for an opening, a breach in the exterior to ooze and seep and spill all over. But it's not the insect Kate's thinking about now.

Taking another glance at her sister's face, at her vacant, staring eyes, eyes that are surely replaying the same gruesome scene as her own, she knows that there will be repercussions for this night.

"You're going to be okay, Lily. Everything's going to be okay."

It's a lie, and she knows it.

FIVE

The hospital has had a facelift since the last time I was here. The medical facility, once an ugly, institutional gray, is hidden from public view on a back road, one you only drive down if that's your destination, so there was no need to be fancy before. Now, the façade is cream colored. A long bank of windows has been installed into the front, a fountain sits amidst a circular drive that loops right up to where an orderly waits like a valet in front of a line of empty wheelchairs.

I have so much trouble finding a parking space that I start thinking that everyone in town must be sick or injured. Then I realize that everyone who's still in town is probably old and in need of constant maintenance. Thus, the fancy makeover.

In the lobby they take our picture and print the image out on a sticker badge for us to wear, complete with our names, the floor, wing, and room number where my mom can be found. We take the elevator up, Lily leading the way. Nurses pass us in the hall, their eyes scanning our badges, making sure we're where we're supposed to be, but not taking the time to look at our faces. Lily stops, standing before the door to my mom's room. She nods for me to go first. I knock lightly and push it open.

My mom is on the bed, dressed as much as she can be with the large cast engulfing her hips. She's smiling, but her face is sallow, her eyes ringed by dark circles. When she sees me, her mask crumples, the fake cheer replaced with relief.

"Mom." Rushing over, I take her hand in mine and brush her hair back from her face. "I'm so sorry. You must have been so stressed, worrying about Lily and how you were going to get home. I should have been here."

She glances over my shoulder to Lily. There's a forced brightness in her tone as she says, "Oh, no, honey. Everything's fine."

Now I know where I get it from. The innate ability to lie.

I settle gently onto the bed beside her as Lily flops into the chair behind me. "What happened?" I ask. "Ms. Lynn said you fell in the shower?"

She averts her gaze, studying our intertwined hands. "It was... nothing. Just a silly accident. Entirely my fault."

"It wasn't nothing," I whisper.

My entire life, this woman's been nothing less than indestructible. Now, she looks weak and frail and much older than the last time I saw her. I try to remember how long it's been, feel my skin flare with heat from the shame.

She gives my hand a squeeze and forces a feeble smile. "I'm going to be just fine, honey. Back on my feet before you know it."

But nothing she says is going to make me feel better, because the truth is staring me in the face. My mom isn't young anymore. Which means she's getting to be the other thing, and I'm not ready for that, not yet.

"Anyways," she says, tone bright. "Now that you're here, what do you say I call the nurse and we see if I can't bribe my way out of here before dinner? I always thought I'd like being waited on hand and foot, but it's no fun when the food sucks."

She winks and gives me a goofy grin as she hits the call

button, pretending like everything's fine, but it's not. It hasn't been for a very long time. As I force a fake smile and try to fit back in with a family I've forgotten how to be a part of, I worry that it may never be fine again.

SIX

When I wake the next morning, it takes me several moments to remember what happened. Sure, I recognize the familiar surroundings of my childhood bedroom, and know where I am, but I've been back within these aqua-colored walls plenty of times over the years in my dreams—and nightmares. And although the light streaming in through the slats in the blinds and the scent of my mom's laundry detergent ground me in reality, it's still disconcerting.

I trudge down the hall feeling hungover even though I didn't have a drink last night. My emotions are taking their toll, leaving me with the stomach-dropping sensation of having ridden a rollercoaster. It tightens into a knot as I pause outside the door, not sure if I should knock.

What's been most shocking about my homecoming so far is how tired my mom looks. I don't want to wake her if she's sleeping. But one of the most awkward lessons you learn as a kid is to knock before you enter your parents' room. I think of all the embarrassing situations that I could walk into unannounced, then realize most of those scenarios are impossible since she's alone and bedbound.

I decide to risk it, turning the handle as silently as I can, cracking the door open just far enough for me to slip my head inside and smell the sweet peach-blossom scent of her room. My mom sits propped against the headboard, awake. Her arms are curled around herself as if she's cold. Her face is blotchy and red, her eyes bloodshot and shiny. It's obvious she's been crying.

"Mom." I push the door open a little farther, reluctant to go inside. "What's wrong?"

She lifts her shell-shocked gaze from the cell phone on the bed beside her and turns toward me, the anguish in her expression so clear that my legs go weak. They tremble beneath me as I push my way into the room and close the distance between us, hurrying to her side.

"Is it the pain? Do I need to call the doctor?"

She sniffs and swipes at her runny nose with the back of her wrist. Her voice wavers when she speaks. "Oh, honey."

"What is it?" I take a step backward, away from the bed. Maybe it's me. Maybe she's trying to find a way to tell me that she wants me to go away. After all, she didn't ask me to come. She never even called me to let me know she was hurt.

She grasps at the sheets, clenching a handful in each fist, her eyes squeezed shut as she struggles to draw several deep breaths.

"Mom. You're scaring me."

"I'm fine. Honestly."

But she's not. Her body shakes like she's holding a cough, and when she finally releases whatever it is she's trying to contain, it's on a sob. Her body shakes violently, tears streaming down her face as she gestures for me to join her on the bed. I do, reluctantly.

"I don't know how to tell you this," she says. She puts a hand on my knee but refuses to meet my worried gaze.

"Just say it," I whisper.

She sighs, the air from someplace deep, the sound so forlorn that the hair on the back of my neck prickles with angst. "This isn't going to be easy to hear."

I was right. It's me.

"It's Emma."

I curl my fingers into the sheets, fighting a wave of dizziness.

"Kate, honey. She's dead."

Her voice breaks over the last word and she starts to cry again. I barely hear it against the sound of the air leaving the room, sucking my lungs dry, imploding my heart. My best friend, my worst fear, is gone. Forever.

SEVEN

I shouldn't be here. My eyes lock on the box at the head of the room. Emma's box. Her coffin. I'm seeing it with my own eyes, and I still don't believe it.

An organist plays in the corner, somber notes floating over the crowd of black-clad mourners to reach its fingers around me at the back of the room, wrapping my body in its embrace like a snake, a constrictor that tightens its hold each time I exhale, making it harder and harder to breathe.

Dim lights cast everything in a yellow hue. Emma hated yellow. She would have hated everything about this, actually. At least the Emma I knew would have. But it's been a very long time since I knew Emma.

I guess a part of me figured that we'd sort everything out one day, make amends, put the past behind us and resume our lives, our friendship, right where we left off. Now we'll never have that chance. Not that it was actually an option, not after what happened, but still...

The only chance left to me now is to go up to that casket, look down inside it at Emma's face, and whisper all the things I never got a chance to say. But to do that, I have to move from this spot, which I'm not sure I can do. My body trembles, a small, uncontrollable muscle reaction that ripples under my skin like a shiver. My legs feel weak.

"Emma would have hated this."

The words, torn from my own mind, tickle my ear. Her shoulder brushes against mine, and for a moment we're teenagers again, slouching in the back of the high school auditorium, snickering at some dumb assembly. Melinda's hand touches mine. Her fingers curl around my fingers, and then somehow we're holding hands like it hasn't been a decade since we last spoke.

I glance at her, catch her eyes, and we share a small smile. She squeezes my hand and looks away, back toward the front of the room. I can't help but notice the suit she's wearing, the designer heels, the expensive jewelry. This is not the Mel I grew up with.

"Geeze, what's with all the geriatrics?"

Becca doesn't bother to lower her voice. Tact was never something she concerned herself with. I guess nothing's changed. Only everything has changed, yet here we are, the three of us, four if you count Emma, which I'm not sure if I should, but figure I might as well. Together again, but for the worst of reasons. In a few hours, Emma will be lowered into the ground. This is the last chance we'll ever have to be together, the four of us.

It's almost like Emma planned it, timed it so that we'd all be here together, again, for the first time since then, that night so long ago. The gang's all here. Only, not really.

Becca sniffs hard, then I feel her against me, her side pressed firmly against mine. Her arm bent across my back. Her hand on my shoulder.

It's that quick. That simple. All it took was for us to be in the same room together and here we are—us again. Without skipping a beat we've fallen back into the comfort of a friendship that was abandoned as long as it existed. We were eighteen the last time we spoke, that night out in the woods where the world as we knew it unraveled, revealing sharp, dangerous edges shining sharply in the harsh glare of reality.

I'm twenty-eight now, too old to live in the fantasy world spun by a teenage mind, too young to be at a funeral for my once closest friend. And yet, as my thoughts are trying to veer toward the smoky haze of my adolescence, here I am, standing in this room at the Bowman's Funeral Home and Crematorium in Wakefield, Florida, where my friend lies in a box at the other end of the room.

A part of me expects to see Emma's head pop up in the coffin any moment now. For her to shout, "Surprise!" her mischievous eyes twinkling, her lopsided smile hanging easily across her face. I want it so badly that I can see it happen, her tightly coiled auburn hair bouncing as she sits up, moving with a life of its own.

And yet, squeezed in between all the heartache and regret and grief, I can't help but feel a sliver of relief. Emma is dead. Maybe that means the nightmare is over. Maybe her death will pave the way for the first step of recovery, make it all right, safe, for me to be back.

"Girls. You came."

The voice, whose timbre scratches at a corner of my memory as being familiar, is spoken by a woman with a face I don't recognize at all. The eyes, though. Something about them.

"Of course, Mrs. Daley."

As soon as Becca says it, I know it's true, but I still can't reconcile the face I see before me with the memory in my mind. The Mrs. Daley I knew was young, beautiful. Nothing like this creature before me, with wrinkles deeply etched into the sallow skin of her thickly powdered face.

Becca withdraws the comfort of her touch from me and offers it to Emma's mother, wrapping the woman's hand between her own. Mel has her hand on Mrs. Daley's shoulder and they're all staring at me, waiting for me to morph the polite smile I reserve for strangers into something more intimate, maybe even say a few words.

"Mrs. Daley." My voice cracks.

Her lips tremble, eyes shining. I have no words. What can I say to this woman who's just lost her daughter? This woman who I used to bake cookies with, who used to braid my hair and paint my nails, who welcomed me as part of her family for years and who I turned my back on so suddenly and for so long that I couldn't even recognize her a moment ago? I throw my arms around her, hugging her tight, painfully shocked by the frail feeling of her bones.

"Oh, Kate."

Pulling back, she presses her lips tight into a sad smile and cups the side of my face in her palm. She looks from me to Mel and Becca. "You all look so grown up. So beautiful."

I wonder if I should compliment her. What would I say? Her once flawless, porcelain skin has been replaced by a spotted piece of parchment so thin that I can see the tubing of her veins, the lines of her tendons lying just beneath the surface. Her glossy mahogany hair is now a thin, brittle gray, her clear eyes now cloudy and yellowed. Suddenly, it's clear to me that life has been unkind to Mrs. Daley for quite some time before the loss of her only child.

Becca clears her throat and says, "How?"

I'm relieved to have the attention transferred from me. Emotions flicker across the older woman's face, a story I can't quite read. It looks like she's battling with herself, debating what to say.

"Emma was out walking. A couple of kids found her, out in the woods by the dunes. She'd somehow, well, they still haven't figured out where she came into contact with the peanut oil, or how. She didn't have her EpiPen."

Now I understand the struggle. With such a severe reaction to such a common substance, Emma always carried an Epi on her. To hear that she wasn't makes me wonder if the oversight was intentional. Her mother couldn't possibly wonder the same thing, could she?

Was Emma's fatal allergic reaction an accident, or something else? The Emma I knew—but then, I didn't really know her, did I? No matter how close I thought we were, there was an entire side of herself that she kept hidden from me. A dark, dangerous side. How deep did the roots of that darkness grow within her? Deep enough to make her kill herself?

Mrs. Daley sniffs once and hastily looks for a reason to retreat.

"I must..." She gestures around the room, and we nod our understanding. "Thank you, girls, for coming today. It really means a lot. Emma... I know it would have made her happy."

"Of course."

My heart breaks all over again as I watch Mrs. Daley shuffle away.

"Wow, what happened to her?" Becca's eyes are opened wide. She's always been overly dramatic. "She used to be so... My mom looks a lot better than that."

"Yeah, mine does, too."

"Yeah, well, I guess we might as well get this over with," Mel says, nodding toward the casket at the front of the room. It's no surprise that she doesn't want to talk about moms. She never has, not that I can blame her. Melinda's mom was, and if she's still alive, no doubt is still, a meth head.

I didn't always know this. When I was little my mom just told me that her mom was sick, and that's why we had to stay away from her. By the time her mom was thirty she looked like a skeletal Halloween prop that had lost half its teeth.

"Kate?"

Shaking my head, I bring myself back to planet Earth.

"Sorry, what were you saying?"

Becca looks at me with concern. "Maybe we shouldn't. Go look, I mean. I can stay here with you if you aren't feeling well."

"No. I'll be fine. I don't think I'll really believe it unless I see for myself. And I'd like a chance to say goodbye."

I move up the aisle, following in Melinda's wake, Becca trailing behind me. Mel stops and waits a few feet before our destination. We spread out along the length of the casket and take the final steps together, as one, and look down.

Emma looks like she's sleeping. Besides some puffiness along her jaw and throat, no doubt from the allergic reaction, her face is peaceful, almost exactly as I remember it. I still don't believe this is real. In my mind I hear Emma's voice. "Just kidding! Got you!"

But it doesn't happen. I want it to so badly that I imagine it a dozen times each minute we stand there. I need her eyes to open. I need for Emma to look at me if only one last time, to absolve me of my guilt.

"Are you ready?"

Becca and Mel have taken a step back. They're ready to leave.

"I just need one more minute with her. Alone."

I try to ignore the sympathy in their eyes as they smile and walk back down the aisle. There's something I've got to do. Taking a deep breath, I prepare myself. When I'm ready, I sneak my hand down into the casket, taking Emma's hand in my own. Her skin feels cold and dry and plasticky.

"Emma, I'm so sorry. I wish I hadn't judged you so hard that night. I wish I had tried harder to get past it and that I had listened to what you had to say and that I hadn't let it come between us and keep us apart so long. I wish a lot of things, but mostly I wish that you were still alive and that we were still friends. I've never stopped loving you. And I never will."

Leaning over, I kiss her forehead, then force myself to walk calmly away from the casket. This isn't a joke. There is no surprise. I will never see my best friend again.

EIGHT

I'm halfway to the floor when I feel a strong arm catch me, wrapping around my back. The room spins as I allow myself to be led over to a chair, still too light-headed to see straight. The arm withdraws as I settle into the seat, but I can still feel the warmth of the body beside me.

"Put your head between your knees. It'll help, I promise."

A large hand helps guide me into the suggested position with surprising gentleness. This is so embarrassing. I open my mouth to say so, but I still can't speak yet.

"Kate! Oh my God. Are you okay?"

I stare at Becca's shoes as she shifts her weight from foot to foot before me.

"She'll be fine. Probably just needs some time to catch her breath."

But that's the thing. I can't. I haven't been able to fill my lungs since I first heard the news about Emma. Now, I'm starting to worry that I'll never be able to breathe right again.

"Maybe she just needs to eat something. Remember how she'd get dizzy when her blood sugar would drop in high school?" This from Mel.

I feel like I'm on display, drawing a crowd. Come one, come all, come see the incredible shrinking girl. Because that's what it feels like. Like I'm going to shrivel up and die.

"Becca, give her a candy bar or something," Mel says.

"What? Why me?"

"You have one, don't you?"

"Well... yeah."

"Well, duh, then."

The hand moves in soothing circles on my back, like my mom used to do when I was sick. Hot breath tickles my ear, the voice low and close as it asks, "Starting to feel a bit better?"

I didn't think I ever would, but since I have the over-whelming urge to take a sideways peek at the man beside me, I realize I must be, so I nod.

"You ready to sit up?"

Another nod, and then the hand moves to my shoulder, a surprisingly intimate gesture from a kind stranger, then I realize this isn't a stranger at all. I find myself in the shadow of a man whose face—but nothing else—vaguely resembles the boy I used to know.

"Why don't you guys see if you can't find her some water?"

Mel looks like she wants to object, but Becca quickly loops an arm through her elbow and guides her away.

"Jimmy?"

"Yep. It's been a while, hasn't it?"

I clear my throat, find my voice. "Ten years," I say softly.

"Ten years," he repeats, shaking his head. "Wow. Well, it's great seeing you, Kate. I just wish it was under better circum-stances."

"Yeah, me too."

"This must be really tough for you. For what it's worth, I'm sorry. Emma was one of a kind. The world just got a little duller, you know?"

I'm not sure that I do, but I can't tell him that. I change the subject instead. "I'm feeling much better now, thank you. If there's somewhere else you need to be…"

"Nope. I'm happy where I am right here. Well, not happy." A flush creeps up his neck, all the way to the top of his ears. "Geez. That did not come out right."

"It's okay. I know what you mean."

He gives me an easy smile. He's always had a nice smile.

"So. Where have you been keeping yourself?"

"I've been in Boston the last few years."

"Boston! So, what, do you drink Sam Adams and root for the Red Sox, now? Summer at the Cape and 'pahk yuh cahr'?"

"Ha, hardly. I spent too much time working to do any of that."

"Yeah, I hear you. Well, I've got to say, I'm glad that you're back."

And it looks like he really is. I drop my gaze, his blue eyes suddenly making me nervous. Making me feel I'm not quite sure what, but whatever it is, I haven't felt it in a very long time. "Yeah, well. I haven't bought weed since high school, so if you think I can hook you up…" I joke.

His laugh is genuine, if startled. "Kate, I'm a cop."

"You're what?"

"A cop. Just made detective last year, actually."

Oh. Shit. Is that why he's here, talking to me? What's taking Becca and Mel so long? I scan the room, searching for a means of escape. "That's… great. Congratulations."

"Relax." He puts a hand on my arm, and even though it shouldn't, it has a calming effect. I feel my pulse slow, the heat that had rushed to my head, starting to make me sweat, dissipate. "Everyone always gets nervous when they find out, but I'm still the same guy I was when you knew me, just a little taller and older, and hopefully a bit wiser."

He forgot fitter, stronger, sexier, and, for someone hiding a secret like mine, more dangerous.

Finally I spot Becca across the room, squeezing through the crowd, trying to balance a paper cup of water. And there's Mel behind her, talking to... is that Jeff? My pulse picks up again, this time for a different reason. His name bubbles up in my throat, propelled by the sensations that only seeing your first—and considering how badly I've screwed up my life, sadly my only—love can evoke.

But before I can speak or act, he's gone, vanishing through the doorway. Of course he wouldn't want to see me. Why would he, after the way I ended things?

"Speaking of which."

Jimmy. I'd forgotten he was even here.

"I've got to get going. Are you sure you're alright?"

"I'm fine."

"Well, it really was great catching up. Hopefully I'll see you around."

"Yeah, maybe."

He stands, a frown briefly creasing his face as he realizes he's lost my attention. He reaches inside his top pocket, withdraws a business card, and hands it to me. "If you ever want to get together, catch up on old times, or anything, whatever you want, give me a call."

I force a smile, shoving the card into my purse. "Sure."

As he crosses the room, stopping to say several goodbyes to Emma's other mourners, he keeps casting backward glances in my direction with something that reads much like disappointment. It makes me wonder how much he knows. And how far he'd go to find out.

NINE

The last time I was in this town, there were no coffee houses. Now I find myself sitting in one of several within a five-mile radius of the cemetery, trying to burn off the chill I just can't shake with a large dose of caffeine.

Across from me, Melinda freshens her lipstick in a hand mirror, then slips both back into her purse. Chanel lipstick, sterling silver compact, and the same Hermes handbag I saw featured on a page in *Vogue* while in the waiting room at the dentist's office last month. A far cry from the girl I grew up with, who wore secondhand Payless shoes and thrift-store bag-sale rags.

Becca stands at the head of the booth, coffee in hand, her eyes darting back and forth as she debates which of us to sit next to. A moment later I'm bounced up off the bench as she settles not too smoothly beside me.

"It's so strange," Becca says. "I haven't seen you guys in like, ages, and then we all land in town at the same time and, well, you know," she lowers her voice to a not-so-quiet whisper, "we're all here for Emma's funeral. It's almost like she planned it somehow."

"That would be so like Emma," Mel says.

Becca's eyes go wide. "You don't think she, you know, did plan it, do you?"

"What? To die from an allergic reaction because we were all in town?" Mel smirks down her nose at Becca. She has the same mean girl smile she used to. I guess she hasn't found a new one to buy yet.

"But you said..."

"I meant it would be like Emma to manage to summon us all here at the same time from the 'great beyond', or some shit like that."

"Oh." Becca pulls the wooden stirrer from her coffee, not noticing that it drips on the table as she turns to me. "What do you think, Kate?"

I shrug. "I think it sounds like something that Emma would have enjoyed talking about. I think she'd get a big kick out of us sitting here giving her credit for it. But I don't think Emma had... passed yet when my mom broke her hip last week."

"So that's why you're here," Mel says, a little sharply.

"Yeah. How about you?"

"I have a business deal I'm working on that's local. I just got into town yesterday."

"Around here? What business?" Becca asks.

Melinda ignores her question. "Why are *you* here, Becca?"

"Um, well. Jason and I are getting a divorce, so I've kinda moved back in with my parents. Oh, I guess you guys don't know. Jason's my husband."

"I think we figured that out."

I shoot Mel a look. *Be nice.* She rolls her eyes at me with exasperation.

"We have two kids. Both boys. Seven and four."

"I'm sorry. It must be hard on you," I say, patting her hand.

The stirrer she's been playing with snaps in half. She frowns down at the pieces.

"It is. But, hey." She turns back to face me, cheeks pink, eyes suddenly bright. "Since you two are here, we can get together and hang out. I mean, gosh, I haven't seen you since graduation."

"Yeah, let's hang out," Melinda mocks. She tosses back the last of her coffee and stands. "Listen, it was nice and all, but as far as I'm concerned, this was a onetime only reunion type of thing. You two are free to get together and reminisce all you want but count me out." Spinning on her Louboutin heels, she heads toward the door.

"Whew, what a relief," I say, loud enough for her to hear. I see her back stiffen. She stops mid-step. She turns back to face me, eyes narrowed.

I kiss my middle finger and waggle it at her, grinning. She tries to fight a smile, her lips pursing hard together until they break into a crooked grin. Shaking her head, she continues toward the door flicking us off over her shoulder. "*Konichiwa*, bitches."

"She really hasn't changed at all, has she?" Becca asks.

"Doesn't seem like it."

"Looks like it, though. She's sure not shy about being loaded, is she?"

"What? You think Mel has money now? Whatever gave you that impression?"

We grin awkwardly at each other. The truth is, I can't wait to get out of here. This booth, this coffee shop, this town; but for now I'll settle on the first two.

The mere idea of meeting up with Becca again makes my stomach churn. I don't want to hurt her feelings. It's nothing against her personally. She seems to be very much like the sweet, naïve girl I once knew.

But just being in this town is enough of a reminder of what happened. Being in her company, and Mel's, is like riding a time-warp back to the way things used to be. Part of me wants it so badly that it's become like a craving I can taste on my tongue, like chocolate.

Only, things can never be like that again, not really. There's a line through the center of my life, a crack torn through, an earth-quake-worn rift that separates the before from the after. The memories of that night make it impossible to return to the before.

"So, what have you been up to all these years? Where do you live? What do you do?" Becca asks.

I glance at her sideways, watch as she fidgets with the pepper shaker, spinning it between her fingers.

"I've been living in Boston the last couple of years. I'm a server at a restaurant on the Long Wharf."

Becca's nose wrinkles as she lifts her face toward me, squinting.

"It's kind of like a pier. It's on the water."

"Oh. Do you like it?"

"Yeah, I guess I kind of do. I mean, for the most part, the people you meet are nice. Interesting. And the money is decent. It would go farther if the cost of living wasn't so high, but I've lived worse places, done worse things."

"Do you wanna trade?"

"Huh?"

"I'll go wait tables in the city, and you can be a twenty-eight-year-old divorced mother of two living at home with her parents."

"Yeah, I'll pass."

Becca sighs and settles her chin into the palm of her hand. "Yeah, I would too, if I could."

"You know, your situation isn't all that bad. You have your kids, and a place to live... the single life isn't all that great."

"Mm-hmm. So that's why you started salivating when you saw Jeff. Didn't think I'd noticed, did you?"

I'm not sure what to say.

"You two were so good together. So happy. I really thought you'd go the distance. What happened there?"

Now I'm really at a loss for words.

She huffs out a lungful of air and looks at me. "It's okay."

"Huh?"

"I know you can't wait to leave. And I know you don't want to hang out with me while you're here taking care of your mother. I understand."

I'm shocked. Becca's never been very perceptive. I guess people do change.

"But you're not the only one who grew up and moved on, you know. Part of me didn't even want to go to Emma's memorial. But then there's this other part of me that you couldn't have kept away, that wishes Mel was still here with us despite being a bitch, and that the three of us were sharing our best Emma stories right now. Ten years without you guys hasn't been enough to erase the memories of the ten years with you. And, it just, it hurts."

"Becca." I reach for her hand.

"Don't." She rolls her eyes up and runs a fingertip beneath her lower lashes. "I'm not trying to make you feel bad. The last thing I want is your sympathy. If I were you, I'd get the hell out of here as quick as I could, too. But I don't have the choice and I'm still trying to figure out how I'm going to survive living here where I'm surrounded by memories that make the wound feel so raw."

"Becca." This time she lets me take her hand. "It's not that I don't want to be around you. And I wish we were here talking about good times with Emma, too, but then there's this other part of me that feels... Well, almost relieved that she's gone. Like it will be easier being back here without her, because it'll make it easier to forget about what happened, and I feel so guilty for that. So damn guilty."

I sniff and dab at the tear that's threatening to break from the corner of my eye.

"I still have nightmares about that night," she whispers, pushing a small smile onto her trembling lips. But her nightmares aren't the same as mine. She doesn't know the full story of what happened. Of what Emma did. "I only went because my mom kept harping on how bad it would have looked if I didn't."

"Why do you think Mel came?" I ask.

"She probably brought too many expensive outfits to wear to her business meetings and she needed another place to show them off."

"Ha. I bet you're right."

We share a smile, and, suddenly, I need to say it out loud. The thought that's been haunting me since I answered the phone to find my mute sister on the other end of the line. I swallow hard, my smile vanishing.

"I'm scared, Becca. Actually, I'm terrified."

Becca's eyes widen. She's blinking rapidly. As she leans closer, I wonder what she thinks it is that I'm going to say, if she thinks I'm going to reveal some dark secret about what happened all those years ago. "Of what?" she asks. "The rapist that's been all over the news?"

"Um, no." I'm ashamed to admit that I have no idea what she's talking about, that I haven't kept up with what's going on in Wakefield, despite my mom and little sister still living here.

"Then what?"

"I'm scared that now that I'm back, that I'll get stuck and I'll be trapped here forever."

"That's not going to happen," she says, leaning back. I can't tell if the tight lines etched across her forehead are from disappointment or relief. I know she was expecting more. The truth is, I can't give it to her. All these years and I've never once shared with anyone my memories of that night.

Sometimes, though, I wish I could. Maybe if I did there'd be a dangerous little sliver of a secret that would allow someone else to be able to make sense of what happened. Other times, though, most of the time, actually, I'm grateful that I can't. How heavy would that weight be, knowing that all this time, somewhere in the recesses of my mind, lurked the clue that could explain the unexplainable?

"How can you be so sure?"

"Because if you're still here after your mom doesn't need you anymore, it'll be my foot you feel on your ass pushing you out of town."

I laugh, and with that single action the rigid shell of tension that has formed beneath my skin dissolves. "Thanks. I think."

"Glad to be of service," she grins.

"Becca?"

"Yeah?"

"I actually would like to hangout while I'm here. If you're okay with that."

"Of course." She smiles, then blanks her face. "Kate?"

"Yeah?"

"Can you remind me? Why were we friends with Mel?"

"Ha. I think it was to scare off all the other bullies."

"Oh, yeah. I bet you're right. Well, hey," she pulls her purse open and rifles around, withdrawing a pen and a scrap of paper, "I really shouldn't push my luck and leave my kids alone with my parents much longer, they're probably all hopped up on sugar bribes by now, but here's my number. Give me a call after you get settled and we'll go out for a drink or something."

"Okay." I smile up at her as she stands. "I will. It was nice seeing you, Becca. Really."

"Yeah, you too. I've missed you."

I watch her walk through the doors and out onto the street, and, like magic, it's immediately easier to breathe. Crumpling the receipt with her number on it, I consider tossing it into the trash before I shove it into my purse. I lied. I am a liar. And if another ten years goes by before I have to see either Becca or Melinda again, it will be too soon.

TEN

They stumble over roots, twist ankles in the soft sand, yet Kate urges her sister to go even faster, like maybe, if they just try hard enough, move quick enough, they can outrun the nightmare. But they can't.

Every time she closes her eyes, she sees Emma standing over Brad's body, the bloodied rock clutched in her hand. Her best friend is a killer. There's no escaping that.

The shadows bunch and gather in the woods, crowding around, making it nearly impossible for her to see. Something rustles in the branches overhead. A night creature. Can it hear the pounding of her pulse? Can it smell her fear?

"I'm sorry, Lily. I'm so sorry," she whispers.

Bile creeps up her throat, is bitter on the back of her tongue, but she doesn't have the time to be sick. She's spotted a dark shadow ahead, a man, quickly approaching. Blocking their escape.

Wrapping an arm around Lily, she hugs her close and pulls them behind a tree. Peeking around the trunk, she watches as the man draws closer, his features slowly coalescing until she recognizes the face. Becca's dad.

What is Mr. Wallace doing out here?

She squeezes her eyes shut, willing them invisible as his heavy steps crash through the woods like a wild animal's. No one can know they're here. No one can find them. There'd be too many questions. She doesn't think she could bring herself to say the answers.

He passes within yards of where they're hiding, causing Kate's breath to catch in her chest. But even once he's by, she can't move. She's frozen, pinned in place by the sound of his ragged voice as he calls his daughter's name, over and over again, voice fading with distance. And then—

His cry is startled, filled with shock and terror and the emotions she herself is feeling. And she knows. He's found the body.

ELEVEN

All it takes is a single instant for an entire world to be changed. A moment for the light to vanish, for life to be extinguished from behind a pair of eyes. That's why the things that scare most people don't mean squat to me. It's the unknowns that terrify me, the horrors that I've yet to encounter, to even consider, that make it hard for me to close my eyes at night.

And, apparently, to keep them closed in the morning.

Sighing, I toss the covers off and haul myself out of bed, giving up on sleep even though I'm exhausted. There's no sense lying here torturing myself when there's so much that needs to be done. Maybe if I focus on helping my mom with her problems, it will keep me from dwelling on my own.

The tiles feel gritty beneath my bare feet as I walk down the hall, and I add sweeping to my to-do list for the day. One more meaningless task that will hopefully keep me too busy to think about all the amends I should be making while I'm here. The thought makes me glance at Lily's room as I'm on my way past, then backtrack and push my ear to the door.

I hear nothing but silence, but I know she's awake. I can feel the energy thrumming through the door. I wish I could knock. I wish I had the strength to pass over the threshold into her room like it was no big deal, to sit on the bed beside her and do sisterly things, to play games like we used to, because she always loved them so much, but I don't. I can't.

The little girl who people called my shadow because I took her everywhere with me no longer exists. She's an adult now. A complete unknown.

Shuffling down the hall, I swallow my remorse, one more bitter pill added to my daily medicine. I tap lightly on my mom's door before opening it and peeking inside. She looks up from the book she's reading and smiles.

"You're up early," she says.

I don't have a response. Instead, I push the door open farther and step inside. "Are you ready to get up?"

"Are you kidding? I have to pee so bad that I was actually contemplating using that thing." She gestures toward the plastic bedpan on the nightstand.

"You can wake me up anytime you need help. That's what I'm here for, you know."

"I know, dear, but I wanted you to get some sleep. You look so... worn out."

"Thanks."

"I didn't mean it like... you know what I'm saying, Kate. Is something bothering you? Have you been sleeping badly?"

I pull the covers off her and help her swing her legs over the side of the bed. I keep my arm around her waist, getting ready to help her stand. Her arm is wrapped around my neck. Our faces are only inches apart.

"It's just... odd. Being back here and all. It makes me feel like a teenager again. That's enough to make anyone tired, right?"

"Hmm." She studies my face. I feel my cheeks grow hot under her gaze. It's like I'm hiding a secret about a crush instead of a murder. "Your sister isn't giving you a hard time, is she?"

"Lily? No, she's been great. Why would you think that?"

"No reason. It's just been a long time since I had both of my girls under one roof. On three?"

"On three," I confirm, counting down and lifting her to her feet. She can't really walk, but can kind of totter from side to side as I inch her across the floor to her bathroom. I look away as she pulls her nightgown up and I help lower her to the toilet.

"I'll need a moment."

"I'll be right outside."

I close the door and slide down against the wall, waiting. It's strange for me to be this intimate with another person, even if it is my mom. Me and Lily, we were once so close. Me and Emma, too. I used to be such a people-person, the overly affectionate girl who was always hugging people. I loved crowds and meeting new people and was never alone.

Now I avoid human contact like the plague. I've had few relationships since high school. There's been a few far-flung nights over the years when I haven't slept alone, but those were always a side effect of drowning my sorrows.

I'm unable to lower the barricade I've erected to let anyone in past acquaintanceship. I tell myself that it's because I'm not interested in more right now, that I enjoy my life and my independence and what many people would find a disturbing amount of solitude, but I know the truth.

The truth is that my ability to trust is broken. Someone who I knew, who I loved, who I was so close to that I would have thought myself able to accurately predict their behavior in any given situation, did something terrible. Something I never would have believed they could do if I hadn't seen it with my own eyes. Hell, I did see it with my own eyes, and I still have trouble believing it.

"Kate?"

My mom's voice sounds hollow through the door.

"Coming."

I rise to my feet, wondering for the millionth time about what goes on in other people's minds. If there's anyone else who, like me, considers everyone a suspect. Mothers, daughters, sisters, brothers—anyone is capable of the unspeakable. How can I be expected to put my heart in the hands of another, to let my guard down, knowing that? The truth is, I can't. And that's why I'm doomed to be alone forever.

TWELVE

Ms. Lynn sits on the couch in the living room, my mother's wheelchair pulled up beside her. I hear them arguing about daytime TV options while I fix them tea in the kitchen. I find the biscotti that came with the gift basket I sent my mom last Christmas and arrange it on a plate. Carrying the refreshments to the living room, I arrive just in time to hear Ms. Lynn say Emma's name.

Both women cast guilty looks in my direction. The annoying clatter of a game show fills the silence. I set the tray down on the table before them and try to make an escape, but I'm not fast enough. Ms. Lynn catches my arm, her withered fingers tightening around my wrist.

"I'm so sorry to hear about Emma, dear. Losing a friend is a shock at any age, but especially when you're as young as you are. I remember what a lovely girl she was. She was here so often that I used to joke with your mother that she had three daughters."

A dark cloud flashes briefly over my mom's face, her gaze darting to the floor. It hadn't occurred to me until now how much Emma's death might be hurting her, too. She'd always been a little standoffish with Em, especially considering how often she was over here, but she was always welcome in our home. I wonder now if maybe my mom sensed something I failed to?

I give Mrs. Lynn a nod, lips pressed tightly together to keep the words from escaping. I force what wants to be said down, pinning it firmly under my tongue.

"Sit." She pats the couch cushion next to her. "Talk with us. It does no good to keep things like this in, dear."

"I'm fine, Ms. Lynn. Really. Emma and I had grown apart. I hadn't talked to her in a very long time."

"That's part of life. It doesn't mean that you stopped caring about an old friend."

"Did you see her mother at the funeral?" my mom asks.

"Briefly."

"Poor Debbie must beside herself," Ms. Lynn says. "Losing a child is unimaginable enough, but under such circumstances. The uncertainty must be eating her alive."

"What circumstances?" I ask. "I thought Emma had an allergic reaction."

"She did."

"Then what is there for Mrs. Daley to wonder about?"

Ms. Lynn and my mom exchange glances. I can see the silent debate going on between them.

"What is it you're not telling me?" I ask.

"Kate." My mom holds out her hand to me. I take it. "Emma was found out in the woods. She didn't have her EpiPen on her."

"I know. Maybe she just forgot."

"Maybe she did. I remember that Emma was very good about always remembering to carry her pen, even as a child, but maybe she did forget. But..."

"What?"

"There have been rumors. That maybe what happened wasn't an accident."

"Are you saying they think Emma killed herself?"

She shrugs, her eyes dropping to her lap.

"That's ridiculous." I take my hand from my mom's, tuck my hair behind my ears. Even though I had considered the idea myself, hearing other people say it is making my heart do a weird flopping thing in my chest.

"I mean, I'm not saying that Emma would never commit suicide, who knows what people have a mind to do, but she wouldn't have done it like that. There's no way. She was terrified of having a reaction. She said it was the scariest thing she had ever experienced. That's why she was so good about remembering to keep an EpiPen on her. There's no way she would have triggered an attack herself."

"That's what everyone keeps telling Debbie, but I guess Emma had been having a hard time lately. I wish that you'd go talk to her, Kate. I know that it's been a while since you and Emma were close, but you were still one of the people who knew her best. I think it would do Debbie a world of good."

My mom stares up at me expectantly. I don't want to do it. I can think of few things I'd like to do less, but a part of me knows that I'll go. Mrs. Daley was a second mother to me, and for the longest time, Emma was my other half. I can't help but feel like I owe this to Emma, for all of the good times.

"Okay."

I'm not sure how to describe the smile that lights my mom's face. It's a smile I've so rarely seen since my dad passed. It makes me feel like I've made the right decision, despite the chill that's wormed icy fingers under my skin. So why do I feel a dire need to escape, to leave this room and this house and the expectations shining in the eyes before me? The shrill ring of the phone rescues me.

"I'll get it."

I dash into the kitchen to answer it, even though the phone on the hall table is closer.

"Hello?"

I decide that the voice on the other end is my new favorite person, stranger or not, as the pharmacist explains that they can't deliver my mom's medication because they don't have it in stock right now. That I'll have to drive to the pharmacy at the hospital to have it filled.

"No, it's no problem. I'll go pick it up. No, no inconvenience at all. Uh-uh. Thank you. Goodbye."

My relief is immediate. Grabbing my mom's keys off the hook, I head back to the living room. My mom and Ms. Lynn are discussing why Emma and I stopped being such close friends, their low voices carrying by a strange feat of acoustics.

"Hey, Mom," I call, pausing a moment to give them time to stop gossiping. Poking my head around the corner, I say, "That was the pharmacy. They don't have your prescription in stock, so I'm going to run up to the hospital to get it filled. Can I get either of you anything while I'm out?"

My mom stares at me for a moment, wide eyed and pink cheeked like a kid caught with their hand in a cookie jar, then recovers herself. "Nothing I can think of."

I turn to Ms. Lynn, who shakes her head.

"Well, I'm off then. Be back soon."

"Drive safe, dear."

I nod, heading out the door to the garage. I wonder what it's like, being one of those people who wears their heart on their sleeve, their emotions plain to read on their face. I wonder how differently my life would have turned out if I were one of them. Luckily, I've learned to be a smooth liar. My best friend left me with no choice.

THIRTEEN

The drive to the hospital goes quickly, but, once again, I'm forced to squeeze my mom's minivan into a spot at the far corner of the parking lot. After hiking across the tarmac under the heat of the rising sun, wading through last night's dew as it rises up in a steamy haze, the hospital feels like a cold, dark cave. I pose for another picture ID badge and am pointed toward a different set of doors. I'm looking at the signs on the wall to see which way to go when I hear my name.

"Kate? Kate Parker?"

My first thought is to run, which is deemed both ridiculous and overly dramatic by my second thought. I plaster my fake server smile across my face and turn, to find myself staring right into a pair of green eyes that I used to lose myself in for hours. How I'd give anything to get lost right now.

"It is you." Full lips curl into a smile. Glossy brown hair sweeps low over his forehead, touching eyebrows with an impish arch.

"Jeff?"

He points to the badge clipped to a pocket on his white jacket.

"It's Doctor Jeff now."

"Wow, I had no idea. Congratulations."

In less than ten seconds I've confirmed that there is no wedding ring, tan line, or indentation on his left ring finger. I'm not quite sure what that says about me. I'm not entirely happy that's the first thing I noticed. But I'm not entirely unhappy, either. I don't get much time to psychoanalyze myself, though, because seconds later I'm one half of a hug that should be awkward, but so isn't, that I melt into the embrace until it is.

"Sorry," I say, pulling away. I feel my cheeks burning and wonder how red they are.

"Don't be."

"It's great to see you. I'm glad to find you've been doing so well."

"Yeah. And you? How are you doing?"

"Oh, I'm hanging in there."

"As good as all that?"

My laugh sounds nervous, immature. "Well, it would be nicer to be here under better circumstances."

His face creases with worry and he glances around like he's just remembered where we are.

"Is everything all right? Lily?"

"My mom. She broke her hip. Nothing too serious. I'm just here to lend a hand while she's healing."

"So, you'll be in town awhile then. Won't your kids miss you? Husband? Boyfriend? Am I being too obvious? I'm being too obvious, aren't I?"

This time my laugh sounds genuine.

"Maybe a bit. But no, there's no one to miss me."

"I find that hard to believe." I feel myself grinning at him like an idiot. I try to chill, take the toothiness of my smile down a notch, but I can't. Apparently, I've lost any skill I ever had at playing it cool. But those eyes. They lean in closer to my own as he says, "You'll have to let me take you out while you're in town. So we can catch up."

He reaches a hand out to my arm and gives it a squeeze, drawing me a little closer. His eyes catch on his watch.

"Oops. I've got to go, I'm late for a consultation. But listen." He reaches into his top pocket and pulls out a notepad and a pen. Turning to a clean sheet, he scribbles quickly and tears the page free, holding it out to me. "My cell number."

Our fingers brush as I take the paper from him. He keeps a grip on it, letting the touch linger.

"And, Kate? I really hope you call."

I watch him walk down the hallway until he rounds a corner, the same purposeful stride he had in high school. Jeff and I started dating during sophomore year. By the time we were seniors, everyone, including myself, assumed we'd be one of those high school couples that make it through college together and get married. Jeff is the future that might have been.

There's no real explanation for what happened between us. It was simply another consequence of that night, the one that changed everything in a single blast, singeing everything familiar, charring everyone I loved, destroying both my heart and my brain with the power of a nuclear explosion.

One minute I was a normal teenager celebrating her high school graduation, the next I was a survivor with only one option, an intense desire that radiated throughout every cell in my body like toxic fallout. Escape.

Less than two weeks later I left behind my friends, my family, my potential college education, even Jeff, like a TV show I used to watch but had changed writers and turned bad. I promised I'd come back, even though I knew I couldn't. Except, here I am. Back. Maybe better late than never.

Shaking the memories from my head, I get my bearings and start down the hall to my left, toward the pharmacy. It feels like

I'm floating. I'd forgotten that I could feel like this. Maybe this trip won't be such a huge disaster after all. Or maybe I'm deluding myself, daring to believe that I'm here for my happy fairy-tale ending instead of my comeuppance.

Rounding the corner, I find my destination. The hospital pharmacy is a long window with wire trapped between two panels of Plexiglas and a roll-down metal door curled above the opening. It looks like a storefront that belongs on a seedy city street, not within a hospital in a sleepy little town.

Approaching the window, I tell the man behind the counter why I'm here. He gives me a long look, just long enough to make me feel like a criminal, then calls my mom's usual pharmacy to confirm that they don't have her prescription in stock. Leaning a shoulder against the wall, I take out my phone and scroll through my email.

"Kate?"

I hear my name spoken for the second time in under an hour. This time, I hope it's meant for someone else. Looking up from my phone, I find myself staring down into Debbie Daley's face.

"Mrs. Daley, how are you today?"

The man who, just a minute ago, I had written off as a jerk, greets Emma's mom with a warm smile. He comes around to the hallway, waits for the door to click shut behind him, and gives her fragile frame a gentle hug.

"I'm fine, Ricky. How are you?"

"I've no complaints, now that you're here. But if you needed your script, we could have arranged to have someone drop it off for you."

"I appreciate that, but I needed some time out away from the house."

I'm shocked at how old she sounds, how much her voice wavers with each word. She looks like she's aged another decade in the day since Emma's funeral. I feel like a voyeur listening to their conversation, even though I'm standing right there with them, three people clustered in a hall.

"Should you be driving?"

It strikes me then that maybe the loss of her daughter isn't the only thing wrong with Mrs. Daley. Looking closer, I now see the telltale signs of disease.

"I took the bus."

"The bus! You definitely shouldn't be taking the bus, not in your immunosuppressed condition. You wait right here while I fill your script and I'll find someone to give you a ride home."

"Well, maybe Kate could do it."

Both sets of eyes land on my face. I feel my skin growing hot under their gazes.

"Only if it's convenient. I wouldn't want to burden you."

"No, not at all. I'd be glad to take you home."

The pharmacist actually leans toward me as he takes a closer look at my face, like he can see the lie on my skin. He studies me for a long, hard minute. Finally, he nods and, punching in a code on the keypad next to the door, lets himself back into the pharmacy. I exhale a breath I hadn't realized I was holding.

Mrs. Daley looks up at me, her jaundiced eyes rheumy, and smiles. Her lips tremble. I can't believe that I didn't notice before how very ill she is.

Debbie Daley had been the epitome of beauty to my younger self. Flawless skin, sparkling bronze eyes, thick, luxuriant hair that should have starred in shampoo commercials. This woman, who is very near my own mother's age, looks at least twenty years older. Her entire body quakes with a continuous tremor. She's wearing a wig. There is no way that Emma would have been selfish enough to purposely leave her mom in this condition.

"Cancer," she says, as if smelling my question in the air.

My heart breaks. I blink back the tears as quickly as I can, but they're winning. One spills over my lower lid and trails down my cheek.

I try to respond, but my voice doesn't work. Clearing my throat, I try again. "What kind?" It comes out in a broken whisper.

"They think it started out as skin, but it had metastasized by the time I was diagnosed. The cost of a life lived under the Florida sun." She shrugs, then her look sharpens. She takes me by the hand and looks intently into my eyes. "You must watch your skin for changes, Kate, and get regular checkups. Emma had just made..."

She stops, sniffs, squeezes my hand before dropping it.

"You girls were horrible about putting your sunscreen on when you were younger. You really need to be vigilant about this, Kate. It's not something to ignore."

I nod, wondering what it was that she was going to say. Emma had just made what? Why would Emma have made anything if she was planning to kill herself? Every second I become more convinced that Emma's death wasn't intentional.

It was an accident, a very tragic, unfortunate accident. I know I need to tell her mom this. I need to let her know how sure I am that Emma didn't leave her on purpose. Before I can say anything, though, the pharmacist is talking as he piles vials of prescriptions onto the counter.

He asks her if she has any questions about the medications before he fills a paper bag with the containers and staples it shut, then pushes it through the hole in the window. He gives me a begrudging look before passing me an orange plastic bottle with my mom's name on the label.

"And your name is Kate?" he asks.

"Yes." I watch him write it down on a pad of paper advertising the latest erectile dysfunction medication.

"Is your last name the same as your mother's? Parker?"

I realize he's speaking overly loud so that Emma's mom can hear what he's saying, so she can let him know if I'm lying. I want to offer him my driver's license, but instead I just nod and say, "Yes."

I tell myself not to take his suspicion personally, that it's a good thing he's being so protective over Mrs. Daley, but something about the man grates on my nerves.

"There's sixty of each, Mrs. Daley. I triple counted, there's not one less."

"I trust you, dear."

"Yeah, well. There are people out there who would do some horrible things to get their hands on those pills. So you be careful."

Suddenly his behavior makes sense, everything except why he thinks I'm one of those people who would steal prescription medication from a cancer patient. Mrs. Daley loops her arm through mine and gives my hand a pat. "Then I suppose I should consider myself fortunate to have such a close friend of the family here to help."

She lifts her chin as she holds his gaze, daring him to challenge her, and I'm reminded of one of the innumerable reasons why I have always loved this woman. It's not just because she was Emma's mom. Or that I spent almost as much time at her house as my own. It's because she always believed the best of me. Even if that was a mistake.

It's not until I've left Emma's mom in a chair in the lobby and I've set off across the sizzling parking lot, now hot enough to fry bacon, that I have a chance to really contemplate what I've learned. Mrs. Daley has cancer. Her prognosis appears terminal. I don't know this for sure, but I suspect it to be true. She's dying.

Would that have been cause for Emma to kill herself? Did she check out so she wouldn't have to watch her mom's condition deteriorate? And what will Mrs. Daley do, now that she's all alone? Who will take care of her?

There was no Mr. Daley. As far as I know, there never had been. Daley was her maiden name. The Mrs. was just a polite way to tiptoe around the fact that she was a single mother in a small, conservative town. I feel a little tickle of fear at the back of my throat, a gentle reminder that, like Mrs. Daley, I'll have no one to take care of me when I'm older. I quickly swallow the thought.

Unlocking the minivan, I pull my shirt off the small of my back, where it's started to stick. It's a futile gesture. As soon as I slide behind the wheel, my body making contact with the leather seat, the back of my shirt is drenched. I brand myself on the seat belt, then scold myself for not remembering my Florida survival skills. Lesson number one—treat every surface like it will burn you.

Starting the vehicle, putting it in reverse, I look behind me both ways, once, twice, and am rewarded the third time as I see a shrunken old man hobble his way from behind the car. Lesson number two—old people and little kids like to congregate in the blind spots behind big, bulky vehicles.

I leave the minivan idling while I hop out to help Mrs. Daley out of the hospital lobby and into the car. Then I remember yet another Florida survival skill. Sweat runs ticklish fingers down across my ribs, but I don't laugh.

The cold, hard truth is that the intense summer heat makes people do crazy things, like it somehow melts the rational part of their brains away, leaving an empty cone in its wake. It makes people unpredictable, dangerous. Lesson number three—anyone can be homicidal, even your closest friend. I learned that lesson the hard way.

Pulling out onto the road, neither of us talk, as if she somehow knows the thoughts running through my mind, slipping and stumbling like they're treading on sand. I wrap my hands tightly around the scorching steering wheel, using the pain to center myself. I need to get my mind in order, and I need to do it quick, because when we get to the end of this ride, I'm going to need to talk. And I have absolutely no idea what I can say without breaking this poor woman's heart even more.

FOURTEEN

I remember the way to Emma's house as well as I remembered the way to my mom's place. I've made the trip there almost as much. But the drive's never been this tense before.

The chaos inside my head is in stark contrast to the utter silence in the car. It's unnerving. I turn toward my passenger and hear the soft gasping of Mrs. Daley's breath. She's sleeping.

I pull into her driveway, the concrete cracked and crowded by weeds. The yard has turned to scrub and dirt. The house before me, a small ranch style built in the 1950s, is in a shocking state of disrepair.

Shingles are missing from the roof. Paint has peeled off the exterior in long strips, the bald patches surrounded by flaking curls that look like some type of mushroom. Algae creeps up the house, reaching toward windows that are so filthy I doubt any sunlight can filter through.

Turning off the engine, I glance at Mrs. Daley from the corners of my eyes. Her skin is ashen, her flesh folding in on itself, filling hollows from the cancer that's eating her from the inside. Her wig is askew, tilted at such an angle that I get a glimpse of the sparse down sprouting from her spotted skull.

I assure myself that she's still breathing, because she looks, well, dead already. Yet at the same time, in repose, with her guard down, I can see a trace of the woman she once was. Her beauty lingers like a ghost, glowing like an aura around her.

She wakes with a start, as if she feels me watching her. I pretend not to notice, acting like I had just turned the car off and I didn't notice she was sleeping. Turning toward her with a smile that I hope doesn't look fake, I say, as cheerfully as I can, "We're here."

She smiles and nods, brows furrowed as she reaches a hand toward her wig. I hop out of the car and circle around the back, giving her time to straighten herself. I have no desire to bear witness to someone grasping at their last shreds of dignity. The idea catches in my belly, forces me to pause for a moment and clutch my gut until the stabbing pain subsides. A part of me is glad that Emma is no longer here to see this.

Opening the door, I slide my hand around her waist to help her down safely. She's lighter than I expected, a mere wisp of flesh and bone. Her feet slide haltingly up the walk, like each step is over uncharted territory and not the same path that has led to the house where she's lived for over twenty years. The keys jingle against each other as she unlocks the door with her shaking hand.

I enter the house reluctantly. It's dark and smells of mildew and ripe garbage. She leads the way to the kitchen, the smell getting stronger, the house getting darker as we proceed. I remember what a cheerful place this used to be, light and airy, with the sun streaming through windows opened just enough to let a breeze in.

The kitchen is dingy. Something moves inside a half full bag of trash, the stench so powerful it makes my stomach clench like I've been punched in the gut. As I get closer I can see that there are maggots inside, writhing together in a tribal dance of gluttony. Mrs. Daley slumps into a chair at the table, her bag of prescriptions clutched in a gnarled hand.

"Let me take this out for you."

Holding my breath, I force myself to keep my eyes open as I pull the bag of trash from its container, knotting it at the top. She smiles up at me. She looks so weak, so tired.

"If it wouldn't be too much bother, could you take the caps off the bottles for me? They put the easy off lids on them, but I still have trouble."

"Of course."

I pop the tops off the vials, leaving them lined up on the kitchen table. Grabbing a trash bag from under the sink, where I remember she used to keep them, I replace the one I've removed. I grab a balled-up plastic grocery bag and head down the hall toward the bathroom. The air at the back of the house gets worse in strata, like different layers of the atmosphere.

I empty the can next to the sink, wondering whether I should throw in a load of wash from the mountain next to the washer while I'm here. Maybe it would be too presumptuous of me, but it's obvious that Mrs. Daley needs some help. And that Emma checked out long before she actually checked out. How could she let her mom live like this?

Gathering the trash bags, I carry them out to the big can around back, then haul the festering cesspool of filth to the curb for trash pickup, wondering if the lungful of rot I just breathed would prove fatal. I head back into the house, a growing list of things that need to be done forming in my mind. It doesn't matter how much time has passed; this woman used to be like a second mother to me. The least I can do is help clean the place up a bit.

I take the sheets off the bed and throw them in the wash. Then I separate a pile from the stack for my next load. I spray down the shower with cleaner and scrub the sink and toilet. I open the window in the bedroom, do some light dusting, and carry a stack of dishes back into the kitchen.

Mrs. Daley's eyes are closed, her mouth slack. She's sleeping again. A part of me, the weaker part, sees this as an opportunity to escape. To slip out undetected before anything unpleasant can ensue. I try to strengthen my resolve, instead focusing my efforts on loading the dishwasher as quickly as I can, wincing as the once quiet machine chugs noisily through its cycles. I watch Mrs. Daley's face for a sign of waking, but there is none.

I change the laundry over, then open the windows in the living room. Scrub a half inch of grime from all the surfaces. Take the throw pillows outside and beat them, push the clutter into neater piles.

Gathering a heap of weathered newspapers into a stack, I tut to myself as I catch the dates, the most recent one already a year old. Surely there's no point in keeping them. Making a snap decision, I put them in front of the door to carry out later for recycling.

By the time I'm finished making the bed, I've made up my mind. I'll find somebody to look in on Mrs. Daley a few times a week, help out with some of the housework. She needs someone. It can't be me.

The longer I'm here, in this house, the stronger the memories get. The stronger the pull from the closed door at the end of the hall. Emma's room. The desire to crack the door open and peek inside is overwhelming. It takes all my will to resist.

That's not entirely true. Fear helps that door stay closed. I'm afraid of what I would find in there. And of what I wouldn't.

Tracking down a pen and a scrap of paper I write a note for Mrs. Daley. Placing it on the table, I consider whispering my confession to her, but decide against it. My unburdening would only cause her pain. I should leave before I do something stupid. I turn. The sight of the front door fills me with relief.

"Don't go."

I feel like I've jumped out of my skin. I hope it didn't look as obvious as it felt. Fixing a smile on my face, I turn to face her. Her eyes leak sorrow as she uses them to beg me to stay. It's a fight I can't win.

"Please, sit."

I take the chair across from her, shoving my jittery legs under the table so she can't see them bounce.

"Thank you for the help. You didn't have to do it. Any of it." Her eyes lift from my face and stare off into nothingness. "You always were a sweet girl. Such a sweet, kind girl."

The words hang between us, static with electricity. When she looks back at me, it's with a strength she didn't have before.

"What happened between you and Emma?"

I open my mouth, but no sound comes out. There's nothing I can say, at least not that she would want to hear. Closing my mouth, I swallow hard, pushing against the knot in my throat.

"I know it was something bad. That Emma... you two were so close. Sisters. If she didn't take her life after whatever she did back then, after losing you, then I damn sure don't believe that she did it now."

Her body shudders. She sobs, but no tears fall. Getting up, I kneel next to her and gently fold her into my arms.

"Emma never would have chosen to leave you, you know that." I stroke the wiry hair of her wig.

"What happened, Kate? What did she do?"

She pulls back, her eyes searching my face, trying to find the answer to her question. It's not something I can give her. It's not something she should have.

Like fog rolling off water, a cloud drops behind her eyes. Her head gives a little shake of disbelief as she looks at me, as if for the first time.

"Kate." She smiles at me, our conversation of a moment ago forgotten. "Your momma raised such good girls. She really did. You and Lily."

I smile back, shame at my relief eroding my spine like acid. "Let me help you to bed, Mrs. Daley."

She nods, allowing me to lift her from the chair. My arms brace as gently as possible around her back, and bear most of her weight as we make our way down the hall. She sits on the edge of the bed and slips her shoes off, nothing more than slippers, really, and I help her draw her legs up onto the mattress. I pull the sheets up under her chin. She catches my hand, holds it to her cheek. If there was any part of me that wasn't broken before, it's shattered now.

"Such good girls. You and Lily." Her head sinks into the pillow, her grip relaxing on my hand. "Don't know what I would have done these last few months without Lily coming by to talk to me. She was the only one to come and keep Emma company all these years, since you left."

Her voice is less than a whisper. Like the scent of rain carried by wind, her words are recognized by my brain. I'm not actually sure that I didn't imagine them. Then she's asleep, her breathing ragged and irregular.

Backing out of the room, I rip my eyes away from her, tugging against a Velcro resistance. Grabbing the stack of newspapers blocking my way, I close the door softly behind me, then race away from the house while I still have a chance.

Climbing into the minivan, I toss the papers onto the passenger seat and jam the key in the ignition. The topmost headline catches my eye, the word homicide in large, bold print. God, death is everywhere I look in this tiny town. There's no escape. It's the straw that finally breaks me.

I melt over the steering wheel not even noticing the heat. My body heaves with sobs, mourning Mrs. Daley. Though life still persists inside the husk of her body, so much of her is already lost.

I can't imagine how it must feel, to have fragmented thoughts and random scraps of memory collide, meshing into a warped reality. Who knows what's going on in Mrs. Daley's head?

Lily hasn't spoken a single word in over ten years, not since that night. It was a symptom of the trauma she experienced, the shock she was forced to suffer because I was a bad sister. I never should have brought her with me that night. It's my second biggest regret.

FIFTEEN

The night has gone still. The trees lurk in the dark, silent shadows waiting to see what will happen next. And though the echo of Mr. Wallace's cry has faded, Kate still hears it, pounding loud and hard against her eardrums.

A scream of her own is lodged within her chest, begging to be released, as the memory again surfaces. Emma holding the rock. Brad, his body an empty shell, staring at a sky he could no longer see. The grisly scene reflected in her baby sister's eyes as Lily stood helplessly nearby, staring in shock and disbelief.

Emma had been a part of her sister's life since the day she was born. She was practically family. Lily adored her. Idolized her. And had then been forced to watch as Emma... what? Brutally murdered their friend?

A sliver of moonlight slips through the canopy above, painting Lily with its pale glow, gilding the perfect curves and planes of her face. Glinting off her glazed eyes. She looks like a doll, beautiful and delicate but also hollow and inanimate, the only sign of life the trail of a lone tear drying on her cheek. Kate brushes it away with her thumb, wishing she could turn back *time, erase the events of the night from their memories. If only that were possible.*

A hand closes around her shoulder, fingers digging deep into the joint and she gasps, the cry strangling in her throat before it can escape. She releases her hold on Lily as she turns, arms raised in front of her face like she's trying to fend off an attack.

"Mel!"

"Ssshh!"

Mel covers Kate's mouth with her palm, silencing her. "We have to hide."

Pulling Mel's hand away from her face, Kate hisses, "Why? What's going on?"

Mel glances over her shoulder, eyes nervously searching the dark around them. "I don't know, but we need to get out of here."

"How?"

"You drove, right?"

Kate nods.

"Then come on."

Looping her arm through Lily's, she falls in line behind Mel, trailing after her. Grateful to have someone else to follow. Someone else to take cover with.

Only, Mel wasn't usually the kind to hide. So what had happened? Why the sudden change?

"Where'd you come from, anyways?"

Mel glances at Kate over her shoulder. "What do you mean?"

Licking her dry lips, her heart skittering in her chest like it's too scared to beat normally, Kate tries to form her question into words. How do you ask someone if they saw something without letting them know you saw it too?

"Have you been in the woods the whole time? Or were you —" she falls quiet as Mr. Wallace's harried voice sounds in the distance, again shouting for Becca, this time with an edge of panic that wasn't there before.

A prickling sensation needles between Kate's shoulder

blades, like she's being watched. Goosebumps spring from the spot, traveling into her arms and down her legs, covering the surface of her skin.

Ahead of her, Mel rubs at the back of her neck as if she, too, has the feeling. She glances at Lily, her expression still blank, unreadable. But Kate knows it's more than a suspicion—they're not alone. Then, behind them, a branch snaps.

SIXTEEN

I've spent the last ten years struggling to keep my head above water, fighting, if not to make sense of what happened, then to at least find my place in it. I can't stand being lost. But that's exactly what I am.

Finding a stack of fast-food napkins in the center console, I wipe my tears and blow my nose, the smell of fry grease clinging to my skin. I take a few of the deep, cleansing breaths I've spent so many years faking, and pull myself together.

Just a few weeks. I only have to maintain this façade for a few weeks, then I can plan my next escape. Maybe out west this time, somewhere farther, where I can disappear into the desert sand and the open sky.

There's not much of me left, but there doesn't have to be. I need only enough to scrape together the appearance of a human being. Pulling the Kate suit tightly over my empty shell, I think about how easy life used to be.

I remember summers at the beach, me and Emma building sandcastles, riding boogie boards, sampling off each other's ice-cream cones as we raced the heat to beat the sticky drip. Humid nights spent lying on our backs on top of the sleeping bags we dragged out to the tent in my backyard, whispering our dreams to the stars. Helping each other get ready for school, for dances, for dates. All my good times include Emma.

She was my rock. My closest companion. As much a part of me as the blood that runs through my veins. Even after all that happened, it's my memories of her that I use to center myself.

Now she's gone, and the memories I have are all I'll ever have. Hopefully, they'll remain enough.

I'm feeling calmer now, temporarily exorcised of my demons. Backing down the drive, I pull the minivan onto the road and head toward my mom's house. Is it weird that I lived there for the first eighteen years of my life, but I don't think of it as home? Or is that just a normal part of the adult process?

Pulling into the garage, I grab my mom's prescription and head into the house, a gust of cold air welcoming me with a chilly hug. I'm immediately assaulted by the blast of the TV blaring through the house. Walking through the empty living room, I turn it down a few notches before heading to the kitchen.

My mom's wheelchair is pulled up to the table. Ms. Lynn sits opposite her. Empty plates lay on the table before them. I glance at the time. 2:12pm.

Guilt splashes at the edges of my empty stomach. I'm here to take care of my mom. Had she been relying on me, she still wouldn't have had lunch. Grabbing a slice of bread from the open loaf on the counter, I nibble at the edges as the two women stare at me expectantly.

"I ran into Emma's mom at the hospital, so I gave her a ride home and helped with some chores."

Ms. Lynn *tsks* and shakes her head. My mom's brows lower, her lips purse.

"How bad was it?"

I feel like the truth would be a betrayal of trust. But whose? Emma's? Her mother's?

"It was a little messy. Where's Lily?" I ask, trying to change the subject. I wonder if she's had lunch. Then I remember that she's an adult now, in charge of feeding herself.

"A little messy? Or a complete disaster?" Ms. Lynn doesn't take the bait, ignoring my question. She stands and takes the plates to the sink, rinses them, and files them in the dishwasher.

Another wave of guilt washes over me. I should have thought to do that. I had always assumed that if I were in the position to take care of someone else, that I'd be decent at it. Apparently, I was wrong.

Ms. Lynn tsks again and faces me, leaning her back against the counter. "We from the Women's Bible Study Group have been taking turns stopping by after Sunday service for months, and she never lets us through the door. The poor thing can barely stand for five minutes at a time, how's she supposed to keep a house up? Especially now? Doesn't do anybody any good, being so prideful."

"I'm sure she has her reasons." My mom's voice is soft, her words whispered like a secret, and in that moment I see something flash behind her eyes that makes me wonder what she knows.

"It was mainly just laundry," I say, trying not to give Ms. Lynn too much ammo for the rumor mill.

"Still."

We fall silent, three women in a kitchen, all absorbed in our own thoughts. The news plays in the background, mere noise until the broadcaster announces an update on the latest in a local homicide. Her words crack through my skull, thundering like the mighty voice of an ancient Greek God, as she reports that police are still looking for leads in the recent murder of a homeless man. A man who'd been found out in the dunes, his head bashed in by a rock.

In that instant, everything changes. I morph from a swimmer treading water to one sinking down into the inky depths of the deep, caught in a vicious undertow. The reporter segues into coverage on a rape case, but I can barely hear her.

I feel myself gasp as I'm drawn under, but I'm not aware that I'm on the floor until my eyes open, hazy vision clearing to reveal Ms. Lynn's face imploding on itself in worry. She's kneeling next to me, her right hand swatting my cheeks.

"I'm fine," I say, my gaze floating past the fluffy white cloud of her hair to my mom's face. Her eyes are wide, the whites bulging. Her hands clench the arms of the wheelchair in a white-knuckled grasp. "Really."

I can tell by the softening of her face, the muscles releasing from a stone sculpture of panic that she wants to believe me. She needs to believe me.

"Honestly, I just moved too fast. Between that and missing lunch, I got light-headed. It's that time of the month."

Ms. Lynn cocks her head at me, then looks over her shoulder at my mom to take her directive. My mom is completely consoled, so quick to jump on the path of least resistance ever since my father died.

"Are you sure you're okay?" Ms. Lynn asks. I nod. She struggles to her feet with a groan. "Well, that's enough excitement for me today. I'm going to go home and take a nap. I suggest you do the same, Maureen."

She gives my mom a stern look and then turns to me, like I should know better than to cause a fuss. I duck my head, afraid she'll see the truth in my eyes if she looks too closely.

"I'll make sure she does," I say as I trail her to the door.

"You might try one yourself," she adds.

I stare at the floor and nod, shutting and locking the door after she squeezes through. Returning to the kitchen, I see that my mom has returned to normal, my little episode, for lack of a better word, already forgotten.

"I think I will lie down for a bit."

"Of course."

I pull the brake on the wheelchair and steer her toward the hall.

"You don't mind?"

"Why would I?"

The question hangs in the air between us, a dark rain cloud that slowly dissipates, revealing what I couldn't see before. She knows something, or at the very least she's had her suspicions. And my reaction to the news broadcast just confirmed something for her. But what?

I tighten my grip on the wheelchair, using it to prop myself up, to keep from doubling over, worried that I might faint again. All those years ago, when I told the police I didn't know what happened that night, I lied. I had seen the bloodied rock clutched in Emma's hand as she stood over Brad's lifeless body. And now, almost ten years to the day after the first murder, there's an identical case on the news.

I should have spoken up. I should have said something.

A vague memory of the headline from one of the old newspapers at the Daley house flashes in my mind. My stomach lurches, turns to liquid.

"Well, if you get lonely..."

"I'll be fine, Mom. I think I'll try and get a bit of rest myself."

This is a lie, just one more twig added to the dangerous pile of brush I hadn't realized I was leaving behind. The one that burst into flames and turned into a raging bonfire when I went away. How could I not have known? How did I manage to ignore what was happening for so long? Surely there must have been a hint of smoke or something that would have clued me in to the inferno that was to come.

I help her into bed. She puts her hand to my cheek, the exact spot that Mrs. Daley touched only hours before. My skin blisters under her touch, burned by the fire that I'd left behind. I force a smile, pull away and retreat, shutting the door behind me.

The truth is, if you stand upwind and keep your back turned, it's easy to ignore the flames. Especially if it's what you want to do.

SEVENTEEN

After I left, my mom would come visit me. In the earlier years, she'd bring Lily with her. Always a different version of my sister, the girl who spoke volumes with her eyes but never a single syllable from between her lips. Timid Lily, preppy Lily, Boho Lily, Goth Lily, an endless parade of personas, worn for a day, a week, a month, then discarded like a pair of disposable contacts. She was just a young girl figuring out who she was, what she wanted to be.

If things were never the same between us, well, considering what I'd taken from her, I figured I deserved it. So it was no surprise that when Lily got older, she stopped coming on the visits. There were plenty of half-plausible excuses, but nothing that ever truly made sense. I assumed it was Lily's decision, that she chose not to see the sister who had ruined her. That's what I did, after all.

I irreparably damaged my sister by dragging her out into the woods with me that night, all because I couldn't wait a couple of hours for my mom to get home before going out to celebrate with my friends. In my stupid, self-centered teenage world, the only person I could see was myself. The only needs I could consider were my own.

And because of that, because of a selfish decision made by a careless older sibling, my little sister saw that murdered body splayed open. Who knows what else she saw? She's never been able to tell me because she hasn't spoken since that night. But until now, I always thought that she'd been safe.

There's no lock on my bedroom door, so I push the chair from the desk under the doorknob and drop my armload of newspaper onto the bed. It only takes a few minutes to confirm my new suspicions as I thumb through the papers. Bile creeps its way up the back of my throat, coating my tongue with the taste of sickness.

I grab my laptop, my mind racing as I wait impatiently for the computer to boot up. I have to go back to see Mrs. Daley. I need to know if what she said was true. But first, I need to make sure I'm not leaping to conclusions.

Emma was sick, that much is clear now. It's possible she just liked reading about other murders. But what if the saved newspapers were something else—like mementos?

I open several browser windows, entering in the details from each newspaper, letting one page load as I type into the next. The words blur as tears fill my eyes. Because every one of the cases that appear in the newspapers happened in the month of June. Every one remains unsolved.

A wave of nausea crashes through my body, leaving me cold and damp with sweat. I'm dizzy, the room around me undulating like a bad acid trip, and I can't seem to catch my breath.

I had told myself that it was better for my sister if I left, but the truth is, I took off because I couldn't handle her silence, I couldn't face the constant reminder of the consequences of my actions. But now there's another truth. Not only did I abandon my baby sister when she was at her most vulnerable—I left her behind with a serial killer.

EIGHTEEN

There's always been a large homeless population in Florida. It tends to thin in the summer months. The heat and rain don't make for the most pleasant living conditions for those without shelter. Yet, as I dig deeper, read closer, I discover that every June a homeless man has lost his life violently in Wakefield, as if in celebration of the anniversary of that night. It's too much to be a coincidence.

That the police seem to have not noticed a pattern can only be explained by the victims. Only in our messed-up society could being homeless somehow translate to having no worth. Can the absence of a family demanding answers, putting pressure on law enforcement to solve a crime, really make such a difference? Apparently, sadly, it can.

All these nameless men, forgotten and discarded. Except for the first. I'll never forget him, and not just because the image of the corpse is branded into my very DNA, but because he was my friend. When I think of Brad Taggert before that night, with his kind eyes and ragged clothes, my heart wrenches like a dishtowel wrung between two fists.

A thought forces its way unbidden into my mind, an idea I'd

never even considered before. Is it possible that he was killed *because* he was my friend? Was his murder a result of some sick kind of competition for my friendship? Was Emma jealous, resentful of having to share my attention?

I shake the thought from my head. It's immediately replaced by his face, gray and slack in death, the top of his head smashed. Jagged edges of skull glowing under the moonlight, blood seeming black, the spongy matter of his brain glistening. Eyes open and staring into nothingness, the face of his killer trapped forever behind their glazed silence.

Even back then I'd have been the first to admit the strangeness of a teenage girl forming a friendship with a homeless man. He was certainly not an acquaintance I would have mentioned to my mom, but there was something about our bond that was real, that transcended the age and class and gender gap.

When Brad and I talked, I wasn't a middle-class teenage girl, and he wasn't a thirty-something homeless man. We were two humans who understood that pain runs deep, that you could try as hard as you could, but you could never really deny who you were at your core. That all the love and good intentions in the world aren't always enough.

My friends failed to see what I saw in Brad. Jeff, especially, was wary of the man in the battered army jacket who was a constant shadow along the fringe of our group, but Brad was capable of things we weren't, and a tentative, symbiotic relationship was formed—we had money, Brad could buy beer.

And though I don't think they ever realized it, Brad provided something else, a watchful eye, an extra layer of bubble wrap to insulate the overprotected, sheltered kids we were from the dangers of the reality that lurked around us.

I met Brad on a day that was like any other, but it was a day that could have easily taken a turn for the worse. I'd been released from school early to drive myself to a doctor's appointment. On the way home, I stopped at a gas station, filling the tank on my mom's minivan.

It was by chance that I ran inside to grab a soda. Lost in my own thoughts, on the way back to the car, I failed to notice the wolves, four men in camouflaged baseball hats and rebel flag shirts, until I was at the center of their pack. Unable to break through the circle they formed around me, blocked from the safety of my vehicle, I was trapped, cheeks burning at the indecency of their words, heart racing, a prey animal at the mercy of the predators.

I'd barely given a glance toward Brad as I'd gone into the gas station. He was just a faceless bum, leaning against the window to absorb some of the coolness leaking from within. I hadn't given him the time of day, hadn't acknowledged his existence, and yet he didn't hesitate to leave his place in the shade, cross the boiling blacktop of the gas station, and put himself at risk to intervene on my behalf.

I've tried not to let my thoughts wander to what could have happened that day if Brad hadn't been there. I've tried not to dwell on the fatherly faces who met my eyes then looked away, not willing to risk the trouble. Of the other women who dashed by, locking themselves in their cars before speeding off. Of the willingness of all those people to just watch, abandoning a girl in danger to secure their own safety. But it comes to me, late at night, in the dark, more than I care to admit.

Brad did step in, though, coming to my rescue, enabling me to get to the minivan and climb inside while the wolves circled him, instead, so the *what ifs* never had a chance to become a reality. Sadly, my first reaction, once safe in my car, was to drive off. Once I was out of harm's way, it wasn't my problem anymore, right? Then the faces of those who'd glanced away flashed through my mind, and I knew I couldn't be like them.

Leaning over, I pushed the passenger door open and, catching Brad's attention as the sharks circled before they attacked, waved him over. Ducking under the arm of one of the aggressors, he jumped into the car beside me. Locking the doors, I tore off out of the parking lot before the rednecks got the idea to follow us.

Later, across a booth from each other at McDonald's, he confessed that he figured that I would leave him behind once I had the chance to escape.

"Then why did you come over and help me?" I remember asking.

"Because it was the right thing to do," he said.

Brad was a decorated war veteran who had once lived a good life in a nice house with a wife and two young sons. But when he'd gotten back from his last tour of duty, he couldn't force himself back into the mould of his former life. He couldn't sleep indoors, too claustrophobic to close his eyes with walls around him that could potentially crumble, fall in, and bury him under the rubble. I suspected that there was more to the story of what happened during his last tour, but I never found the courage to ask.

Brad slept in a tent in the backyard while his family slept inside for the first year after he returned. He went to work during the day, anxiety building from morning until late after-noon, when he was released back into the wild, as he described it. He told me briefly about how his inability to get back to what his wife described as "normal" stressed their relationship, about how, as his sons grew a little older, they and his friends thought he was weird.

He didn't want to ruin their chance to fit in with society. His wife deserved a better husband, their kids a better dad, and he didn't have it in him to force himself to be something he wasn't anymore.

When Brad told me how his wife had another man living in their house less than two months after their divorce, a part of me wondered how a woman could so easily turn her back on the father of her sons, whose only crime was to be a hero fallen from grace. Then there was the other part of me, the part that completely understood. The part of me that, like the people who had looked away as the men bullied me, had the initial instinct to leave the man who had come to my aid behind. The part of me that I was only just starting to understand as I took my tentative steps toward adulthood.

I was at a crossroads in the life that I was only just beginning. I stood on the edge of a cliff, faced with making the decision of which way I wanted to leap, what type of person I wanted to become, and the crazy thing was, as far as I could see, I was the only one going through it. None of my friends seemed to be stumbling under the weight of the same decisions. They didn't even seem to recognize that there were decisions to be made.

Brad was like a guardian, an angel sent to guide me on my journey. He somehow sensed the precarious ledge I was walking, and while he refused to give me a nudge one way or another, in the months following our meeting he was always happy to lend me an ear and be my sounding board while I felt my own way out of the box.

It pains me that I failed Brad. As I stood over his body that night, the moon at my back, my shadow lost among the copse of trees where the orange grove met the woods, I took my first step in the wrong direction. And I've been running that way ever since.

But now that I know there were more victims, more deaths I may have been able to prevent, I can't let this rest. It's time to take a step back in the right direction. I need to know why. It's the only way I'll ever have a chance to forgive myself.

Something about the open page on the computer screen taunts me. It's the most recent crime, the one I heard the newscast for. The crime that so exactly mirrors what happened to Brad. Was it supposed to be some kind of sick gift?

Surprise! Welcome home! Look what I've been doing all this time while you were gone.

If that's the case, then this is my fault. All of it. Which means I have just as much blood on my hands as she did on hers.

NINETEEN

Suddenly, I understand what Brad used to talk about when he spoke of the walls feeling like they're closing in. I shut the computer down. I need some air. Fast.

Stumbling through the house, I'm gasping by the time I burst through the front door into the glaring heat of the day. My blood has thickened from my time up north, immediately feels like it's boiling just under my flesh. Sweat sizzles on my skin. The hot air feels heavy and wet. I'm already drenched, but I need to get out of here. I need to move.

I walk, gaining speed until the wilted leaves and browning grass are just a blur. I push myself faster, breaking through the clouds of gnats and buzzing mosquitoes that swarm through the muggy heat, but I'm still not moving fast enough. My stride breaks into a jerky gait, knees lifting, arms pumping.

I have never been a runner. I've always been too awkward. My knees knock, my ankles wobble, my heart beats like an angry tribal drum calling all eyes to the sacrificial victim on the edge of a volcano. I couldn't even do the mile run in under twenty minutes in grade school. Yet here I am now. Running.

The legs underneath me don't feel like my own. They

pump harder and harder, beating against the ground faster and faster, but not fast enough. Never fast enough. Because I am the one I need to get away from. I can't outrun myself.

The realization makes my body jerk to a halt, like I've hit an invisible wall. Crumpling forward, hands on my knees, I try desperately to catch my breath. I can't tell the sweat from the tears pouring down my face, hitting the sidewalk between my feet in heavy drops.

I don't hear the car over the rush of the blood behind my ears, but I do feel the vibrations, the heat radiating off the side as it pulls to a stop beside me. Gasping in a deep breath, I hold it, trying to pull myself together to tell whatever creep has pulled up alongside me to get lost.

The window lowers with a mechanical hum. Adrenaline surges beneath the surface of my overheated skin. Part of me imagines taking flight, lifting into the air like a bird, escaping the madness of this earth. The other part of me plans a more realistic escape.

"Kate?"

I hear the voice and every thought in my brain gets sucked away, like tub water pulled down the drain. Looking up, my eyes meet Jeff's. A crack of thunder bellows and the heavens open up, releasing a surge of surprisingly cold rain. Jeff leans across his car and pushes the passenger door open.

"Get in."

I do, already thoroughly chilled, feeling like a hot mess as I shove a wet hank of hair behind my ear before wrapping my arms across my chest, a small act of modesty. Jeff turns the AC off, reaches in the back, tugs a white medical coat from the back seat and passes it to me before putting the car into drive and pulling away from the curb.

I have no idea where he is going. I don't ask. Instead, I lean my head back against the headrest and close my eyes, grateful to pass the reins of control over to someone else. My mind is an empty void, not even a pebble inside to rattle around as the car bumps over the pockmarked road. My body limply rolls with the jolts.

I'm not sure how much time has passed when the car stops moving. It could have been minutes or hours. The engine shuts off and I open my eyes. I wonder if I fell asleep. I wonder if I smell like sweat. I wonder where Jeff has taken me.

The rain has stopped. Gazing numbly out the water-streaked window, I don't recognize the neighborhood. There's not a midcentury modern, ranch, or Spanish style house in sight. I stare at the two-story craftsman in front of me, wondering exactly how long Jeff drove for. How far north could we have gotten?

Jeff pulls the passenger door open, and that tiny seed of hope, that I've been taken far away from my problems, is smothered under the humidity that rushes to meet me. Still in Florida. He holds out his hand. It takes me a minute of staring at it to realize why.

I unbuckle the seat belt I don't remember putting on and slip my hand into his, letting him help me from the car. He keeps my palm in his as I follow him up the front walk, his flesh a small, cool patch in a quilt of sweltering heat.

He lets me go to unlock the door, then steps back, gesturing for me to go inside first. I do. Only the tiniest whisper from my brain questions whether this is smart.

I stand just inside the threshold, dripping onto what I think are real travertine tiles. Jeff leans close, dropping his keys onto a marble-topped table behind me. As he draws back, his body heat is like a cloud, slowly dissipating. I absorb what I can from it, then shiver, realizing how cold I am now that we're inside.

"I'll get you some dry clothes to change into," he says, disappearing down the hall.

I stay where I am, not sure if I'm supposed to follow or not until he reappears from around the corner of the wall, beckoning me. My shoes make soggy squelching sounds as I cross the foyer, tiny prisms from the crystal chandelier dancing across my skin like pixies. By the time I catch up to Jeff, he has an armful of clothes for me.

"Here." He awkwardly pushes them into my arms. "There are towels in the bathroom." His head nods toward the door beside us. "Take a shower. It'll warm you up. The laundry room is next door. We can put your clothes in the dryer, or we can wash them first, if you want."

Reaching out, I give his arm a soft squeeze that gets his eyes to meet mine. Pushing a smile to my lips, I whisper, "Thanks."

"I'll make some coffee. Do you drink coffee?"

I nod and watch him hurry in what I guess is the direction of the kitchen before stepping into the bathroom and shutting the door. Turning the hot water on full blast, I peel off my wet clothes, put them in the sink, test the water temperature with my hand, then step under the delightfully violent flow.

The water kneads out knots I didn't know I had, the flesh of my neck and shoulders softening. I wash my hair with shampoo that smells exactly like what Jeff's hair has always smelled like, ripe green apples on a perfect summer day. It's funny, how you can know so much about someone, yet so little.

Jeff knows my first memory as a toddler, the name of my imaginary friend from childhood, that my hatred of mayonnaise is so deep that it keeps me from trying any white condiment, but he doesn't know how I take my coffee.

I know how Jeff got the tiny scar that runs through his left eyebrow, that he went to speech therapy for five years before he could pronounce his Rs correctly, that he was actually relieved when his parents got a divorce, but I don't know anything about the last decade of his life.

Has he ever been married? Does he have kids? Does he still like watching crappy horror movies and playing board games?

How much have each of us changed over the past ten years?

It's probably foolish to assume that we're still compatible, stupider still to think that we could pick up where we left off as teenagers, but the part of me that's still alive, the small sliver that has yet to be crushed under the weight of the secret I bear, wants nothing more than that.

Turning the water off, I towel dry and pull on the white T-shirt, maroon sweatshirt, gray track pants, and tube socks that Jeff gave me. They make me feel small, but safer than I've felt since the day I left all those years ago. I need to proceed with caution. Jeff and I both do.

I toss my wet clothes in the dryer next door, then follow the delicious aroma of coffee into the kitchen. The granite and stainless steel are a far cry from the peeling linoleum counter-tops and harvest-gold appliances I left behind in Boston.

Jeff jumps up from the round hardwood table, pulls a mug from a shaker style cabinet and fills it with coffee.

"Creamer? Sugar? I might have some milk, somewhere, but I can't guarantee how fresh it is."

"Creamer, please."

He grabs a container from the fridge and hands it to me, setting the mug down before me. I splash enough in to lighten the coffee to the right shade and take a sip, closing my eyes as the hot liquid floods through my system. When they open again, I find Jeff staring at me, a small, quizzical smile bending the corners of his lips. I smile back.

"You look better."

"I feel better."

"So..." The left corner of his lip hitches up into the lopsided smile that always made my heart feel like it was doing cart-wheels in my chest. Besides a few creases at the corners of his eyes, and a line lightly etched like an opening parenthesis at the top of his smile, he looks exactly the same as he used to. My cheeks flood with warmth and my heart goes for gymnastics gold. Apparently, his smile still has the same effect on me that it did in high school. "Running. You run now. When did that happen?"

The warmth in my cheeks flames to a full-on searing fire. I take a long sip of coffee, buying time to gain some composure before answering.

"Just today, actually."

"Really?"

"Uh-uh."

He shifts his weight, the chair legs scraping across the floor under him. He catches my eyes again, holding my gaze. The smile is gone.

"Kate, I'm glad you're back."

I swallow hard. It feels like there's a baseball-sized lump in my throat.

"But…" He shifts again, this time leaning farther over the table, closer to me. "I don't like seeing you like this. Something's bothering you. Maybe something you heard…"

His eyes widen as they search mine. I give the slightest shake of my head. The tension in his body slackens, his shoulders dropping from where they had wrenched up under his ears. Am I kidding myself that he feels relief?

His hand slides over mine. The electricity that zings through me shoves out all other thoughts. This is what it's like to feel alive. I'd almost forgotten.

"Then if it's something about being back home that's got you all worked up, if you're feeling guilty or—"

My hand involuntarily snatches away from his at the g-word. I stare at it, pale and limp on the table before me. For the second time today, I feel the overwhelming urge to run.

"Kate, look at me."

My eyes betray me.

"You took off. Whatever. We all moved on and got past that. Me. Your mom. Lily. Emma."

I can see when he realizes that he's found the head of the nail.

"Emma was happy you got away from here."

"How would you know?"

His gaze drops to the table. I can hear him gulp across the table. When he speaks, it's reluctantly. "We... hung out for a while. When I moved back after finishing my residency."

"Hung out? You mean dated?" It's impossible to believe how much this hurts, even though the rational part of my brain, hidden deep in the shadowy, cobwebbed corner that doesn't get much use, knows I have no right to be so wounded. I was the one that left them behind.

"I had wondered if someone might have told you already. And I wouldn't say dating, exactly. Nothing really happened between us. It was more like we were, I don't know, like we were using each other to feel closer to you. To not miss you as much. I guess it was like we understood what the other was feeling. Does that make any sense?"

The words hang in the air a moment before settling heavily on the surfaces of the room, like sawdust. I shrug, unwilling to speak.

"Anyways. She's gone now."

I give him a sharp look.

He holds a hand up. "Don't get me wrong, we'll all miss her, but maybe, you know... what happened was for the best."

"How so?"

He sighs loudly, rubbing a palm over his face. When he drops his hand, he looks older, a little haggard around the edges. My mind and my body are at odds. I have to stop myself from going to him, offering myself as comfort.

"I was there. When they brought her into the ER. I saw her name come up on the board when the paramedics called on their way in and I went to see if there was anything I could do, but it was too late. She made sure of that."

"What are you saying, Jeff? Are you suggesting that Emma killed herself?"

Jeff turns so I can't see his face. "I don't know if anyone's told you yet, but her mother is dying. Cancer. It had metastasized by the time they caught it. It's everywhere. She doesn't have long left."

I take my time, choosing my words carefully. "The Emma I knew wouldn't have done that. Left her mother to die alone."

He glances at me sidewise, then looks anywhere but me. Rubbing the back of his neck, he says, "You sound pretty sure of yourself."

"Why wouldn't I?"

"People change, Kate. It's been a long time since the two of you were friends. Maybe you didn't know Emma as well as you thought."

"Uh-uh." Even though he has a point, I refuse to accept it. "There's no way."

"You're not going to listen to me about this, are you?"

I don't answer, instead dropping my eyes to the table to avoid his stony stare. We both sip from our cups, the silence growing loud between us. There's so much to say, so much to leave unsaid that neither of us can find the right words to begin. Finally, Jeff clears his throat.

"I guess I should probably drive you home now."

TWENTY

My dry clothes feel too tight after wearing Jeff's things, like a Kate costume that I've outgrown. The drive to my mom's house is tense. I sneak glances at the side of Jeff's face, but his expression is unreadable.

Playing our conversation back through my mind, I suppose he does have cause to be mad at me. He's interacted with Emma much more recently than I have. Maybe he knows her better. And the old me never would have disagreed with him like that.

But I'm not the girl I once was. I'm not the girl he knew.

I'm not sure if the woman I've become is a person I can be proud of. Until a few days ago, I had thought I was okay. Independent, at least. But now it seems like it was just a role I was playing, a persona I adopted, the façade I showed to the world.

Here, among people who know me, or at least who I once was, there's no faking it. I can't get away with pretending anymore. I need to find out who it is that I am.

Outside the window, my old neighborhood rolls by. For the first time, I notice how shabby it looks. Bare patches of dirt overtaking the grass. Fence boards beyond weathered, darkened more by rot than the passage of time. An angry-looking storm cloud hovers on the horizon. If the scene were a photograph it would be developed in black and white and would perfectly portray desolation and loneliness.

Jeff pulls into the driveway and puts the car in park, then turns to face me. I want to trace the curve of his frown with my fingers, smooth away the creases in his forehead with my lips. I want to undo all the sadness and hurt I've caused, but there's so much. It would be easier to be someone else instead. Like I was just less than two weeks ago.

"Kate." His voice breaks. He clears his throat and tries again. "I really am glad you're back. I know it can't be easy for you after being away so long."

He looks out the window, eyes drawn by a hawk soaring low in the sky before us. It lands on a telephone post, puffs itself up before it preens the feathers under its wing.

"I'd like to see you again. But I know you've got a lot to figure out first, so..." His head swings toward me. He looks like a little boy who's just lost his dog. "The ball's in your court."

"Jeff, I..."

He swallows, his jaw squaring into stone. My voice strangles and dies off in my throat. There are no words good enough for me to offer him.

A tear escapes and races down my cheek, tickles my neck. I unbuckle my seat belt and open the door, pausing to gather the strength to step outside. I close my eyes again and take a deep breath, filling my lungs with the scent of this moment, hoping it's not my last with him.

I'm so tired of being alone. I miss what we once had. "I am trying," I whisper.

I pull myself to my feet and close the door without seeing his reaction, my mind screaming the words I should have said instead. Regret chases me up the walk and into the house, but as soon as the door is closed behind me, I feel something else. Relief.

My phone rings, buzzing in my pocket like an angry bee. I fumble it free, hit the green phone icon to take the call before it goes to voicemail.

"Hello?"

"Screw it."

"Jeff?"

"Forget what I just said. I need to see you again. Say you'll go to dinner with me tomorrow night."

"Jeff, I—"

"I'll pick you up at six. Say yes."

"But—"

"Say yes, Kate."

I think of my mom and Ms. Lynn, no one to keep them company but each other. I don't want that to be me in twenty years. So I do it. I say yes.

TWENTY-ONE

A branch snaps, the crack like a gunshot. Mel stops and spins, confronting Kate with wide eyes.

"What was that? Was that you?"

Kate doesn't answer, instead forcing herself to turn, to face the danger. A form emerges from the shadows, barrels toward them.

"Oh, shit," Mel whimpers.

Kate's bladder twinges, begging to be released as she forces herself to stand her ground.

"Dude. Where have you guys been?"

"Becca?" Kate feels herself deflate with relief. Watches numbly as Mel steps forward and shoves Becca so hard she stumbles back several steps, almost falling.

"What was that for?"

"What the hell do you think you're doing?"

Becca rubs at her shoulder where Mel hit her, an injured look on her face. Her dad's voice calls her name once more.

Mel huffs, throwing her hands up in the air. "Why aren't you answering him instead of sneaking up on us?"

Becca's injured expression turns to alarm. "Are you kidding?"

"Why not?" Kate asks.

"He obviously knows you're out here, dumbass," Mel says.

"I just don't want to, okay."

Mel swats at a mosquito on her shoulder, scratches at the bite. "What's the big deal, anyway? You were allowed to come out tonight, right?"

"Yeah."

"So if he's out here, there must be a reason. How do you know something bad didn't happen at home?"

Becca's gaze drops to her feet. She chews on a nail. The finger's still in her mouth, blurring her words as she says, "I just, I wanna stay here with you guys, okay?"

Mel crosses her arms. "Well, we can't stay out here forever."

"What was the plan before I found you?"

"To get to Kate's car. Drive out of here."

"Why can't we still do that now? Are we even going the right way?"

Both girls turn questioning looks to Kate. She pulls at the collar of her T-shirt. "I don't know. It's possible we might have gotten turned around."

"Hey, Lil, can you help us out here?" Mel asks. "You know all that astronomy find-your-way-by-the-stars crap, don't you?"

Lily doesn't respond.

Mel leans forward, peering through the dark at the younger girl. She shifts her gaze to Kate. "Is she okay? She looks—"

"She's fine," Kate snaps. Ignoring the glance her friends exchange, she snatches Lily by the arm, rougher than intended. "Let's go, Lily."

She tugs her sister forward, back into motion.

"Hey?" Becca's voice sounds young, scared. "How do you know you're going the right way?"

Mr. Wallace shouts Becca's name again, this time frantic.

"I don't," Kate says. But she does. She just has to head away from Becca's dad and the nightmare that he found. The one that she and Lily—and Emma—had left behind.

TWENTY-TWO

There's this thing called sleep. I remember it. I miss it. But I can't, for the life of me, find it.

Every time I close my eyes, I'm transported back to that night. When my eyes are open, the faces of all the men I could have saved float before me. It's a losing situation. And I don't deserve any better. Not when I have the blood of nine men on my hands.

I'm just as responsible for their deaths as I would be had I been the one to pull the trigger, so to speak. Because I should have spoken up. I should have done something. Because sometimes, inaction is just as bad as the action itself. I can't believe I was so naïve.

The next morning, I feel like I'm wearing lead boots as I roll my mom up to the table, across from Lily for breakfast. Lily takes one look at me and hops up, throwing her arms around me, holding tight. I cling back like she's a life preserver and I'm lost at sea. For the first time it really hits me that maybe I don't have to do this alone anymore.

I'm not the only one struggling to keep my head above water. True, I haven't been there for my sister in a very long while, but I'm here now. And the squeeze I give her back is a promise. We'll get through this. Together.

Only, even as I make the silent vow to my sister, a part of me is already pulling away, thinking of something else. The wedge that drove us apart in the first place. Emma.

Even though she had done something horrible, a part of me had still missed her. Still loved her. Had hoped that there might eventually be some way for us to move beyond what she'd done. But that was before I learned about the other murders. Because that's changed everything.

If I'm ever going to get past this, if I'm ever going to have any hope of living a normal life in the future, then I need to somehow reconcile the girl I thought I knew with the monster she became. And for that, I need to know why. What was so wrong with her that she felt the need to kill over and over again? And how had I missed it?

Lily grins at me across the table as our mom chatters about her plans for the day, a marathon of her favorite true crime series that she and Ms. Lynn plan to binge watch on Netflix. I force myself to return the smile. Mom's always been a crime buff. If you ever needed to get away with murder, she'd be the one to turn to. She missed her calling—she should have gone into criminal law instead of corporate. I don't think Ms. Lynn quite knows what she's in for.

My sister takes her dishes to the sink, rinses them and puts them in the dishwasher, and I'm reminded—she's not a little girl anymore. Maybe I should confide in her. She might be able to help. This could be something we do together.

But then, on the way out of the kitchen, she pauses. Our mom flinches as Lily surprises her, putting a hand on her shoulder and giving her a kiss on the cheek, an unexpected moment of affection, and I see her as she was then—young, sweet, innocent—and I know this isn't something I can involve her in. She'll always be my baby sister. She'll always be mine to protect. I've failed for a very long time, but that ends now. I can't put her at risk. I've done enough of that already.

My throat squeezes tight with emotion. I struggle to swallow the mouthful of cereal I'd been chewing, pushing hard against the memories threatening to choke me, but it won't pass. I jump up and rush to the sink as I start coughing.

"You okay, dear?" Mom asks. She casts a worried look toward Lily, who's paused in the doorway, her brows furrowed in concern. She looks so unlike the carefree little girl she once was. I need to find a way to erase the damage I've caused.

"Fine. Just went down the wrong pipe."

I wipe tears from my eyes. Run the water to wash the half-chewed food down the drain. I feel like my hope is going with it. All the good intentions in the world mean nothing if you don't act. And I have no idea where to begin. I need a plan.

Emma's dead. Over a decade has passed since the original crime—like the cases in my mom's shows, it's gone ice cold. Lily's not talking, in any sense of the word.

I need a place to start, a ledge just wide enough for me to get a grip on. I need to find out exactly what happened the day Emma died. Then I'll work my way back in time from there.

But I'm too afraid to do it alone.

I need someone to help me, but there's no one. For so many years I thought being on my own would keep me safe. If I didn't let anyone in, there'd be no one to break my trust. I realize now that I wasn't being tough, or smart. Instead, I've made myself weak and vulnerable.

I have no real friends, and while Jeff and I are reconnecting, whatever we have is still in the early stages. Even if I could work up the nerve to make myself ask him for help, I don't want to. Old habits die hard, I guess.

Then I remember the card abandoned somewhere in my purse. A person I can talk to. Someone who wouldn't be doing me a favor, but his job. I need to talk to Jimmy Sutton.

TWENTY-THREE

The heat is already overwhelming, wrapping itself around me as soon as I step out the front door, squeezing me like a boa constrictor trying to wring sweat from my pores. By the time I finagle my mom's minivan into one of the minuscule parking spots at the Wakefield Police Department, the interior of the car has only just become a comfortable temperature. I stare at the heat waves radiating up from the blacktop, a wavering omen of what's to come, then step outside into the oven.

My shirt is damp when I enter the frigid lobby of the police department. It feels like being flash frozen. I stand to the side, trying to ignore my discomfort, reading posters about drug statistics while I wait for the overly nice receptionist to see if Detective Sutton is free to talk.

A moment later, I find myself once again trying to reconcile the face of the man before me with the boy I used to know. The resemblance is there, but as he strides across the lobby to meet me, all strength and confidence, it's obvious that he's changed. It makes me nervous, doubting my decision to come.

Then his lips spread into that easy smile of his, his blue eyes crinkling at the corners, and I forget any misgivings I might have

had. I wonder if he has this effect on the suspects he interro-
gates, instantly putting them at ease. Making them feel safe.
Secure. Like they could spill their darkest secrets and unburden
their soul and he would never judge them.

"Kate." There's an awkward moment where we just stand
in front of each other, where I don't know whether to give him a
hug or shake his hand or what. His eyes scan my face, reading
me like I'm one of the posters on the wall.

He gives a nod and motions toward some chairs in the far
corner, and we take a seat. "Not that it's not great to see you," he
says, voice lowered. He casts a glance at the receptionist, makes
sure she's not paying attention to us, then adds, "But something
tells me this isn't a social visit."

I shake my head, lips pressed tightly together.

"So, what can I help you with, then?"

My nerve wavers. "You're going to think I'm crazy."

His expression softens and I imagine how good he must be
at his job, especially at handling victims. "Why don't you try
me?" he asks.

Taking a deep breath, I brace myself and spit it out. "I think
Emma was a serial killer."

He leans closer to me, putting a hand on my arm to stop me.
"Kate, are you feeling—"

"Jimmy, she was a murderer."

"Listen, I know you're upset. And everyone handles their
grief differently, I get that. Maybe thinking that Emma was a
bad person makes it easier for you to deal with her loss, and if
that's the case, I'm not going to stop you from telling yourself
whatever it is that helps you through this, but you can't make
accusations like that. Especially not to cops. Emma's memory
deserves better than that."

"I knew you wouldn't believe me."

"Kate," his voice is gentle. "It's not that I don't believe you.
It's just that, well, for starters, Emma was a sweetheart. She

wouldn't even hurt a bug. Seriously, I've seen her carry spiders outside instead of killing them. Why would you think she'd have it in her to kill a person?"

I swallow hard, trying to erase the taste of shame from my mouth. "There's something I never told you. Or anyone. About that night. You know... back—"

"Yeah," he interrupts, gaze narrowed on my face. "I know which one."

"I saw Emma. Standing over Brad, holding the rock that had been used to kill him."

"What?" He yelps like he's been stung. Glances nervously around the lobby as sweat breaks out along his hairline, beads on his upper lip. His skin has turned a sickly shade of gray.

"I saw—"

"Yeah, I heard what you said. I just don't believe it. I can't."

"You think I'm lying?" My voice gets higher with each syllable, until I squeak out the last word. I should have known better than to come here. Than to trust him. Or anyone, really.

His mouth twists into a knot as he studies me. Finally, he says, "I think that you believe it's the truth."

I huff air nosily and roll my eyes. "Gee, thanks."

"Kate, I'm not trying to upset you. Really. It's just, I mean, we're talking about Emma here. There's just no way."

"I would have thought the same thing, too, if I hadn't seen it with my own eyes. If I couldn't *still* see it any time I shut them."

Jimmy's mouth is open, jaw slack. His eyes have gone droopy and sad, like the plastic dog that sits on counters by cash registers, collecting donations for the Humane Society. His voice is soft and cautious, his words reluctant as he says, "That's why you left, isn't it?"

"Yes. But there's more." He looks like he's going to be sick, but I press on anyways. "Since I've come back, I've discovered that a homeless man has been killed out where we were in the dunes every year at this time."

He drags a hand over his face, staring off into space as he asks, "Every year?"

"Yes."

He gulps so hard I can hear it. "But you don't really think that Emma..."

I nod. "I don't want to, but what other explanation is there? If it wasn't always the same time of year, or in the same place, then maybe—"

"But that could just be a coincidence. Wakefield isn't the same small, sleepy town that we grew up in. The population's almost tripled since you left. Unfortunately, more people means more crime."

"Maybe some of the murders were a coincidence." I decide not to tell him about the newspapers I found at Emma's house just yet. Baby steps. I need him to see a connection before I overwhelm him with details. "But I saw a report on the news. About a recent case. And it sounds like it was almost identical."

He rubs the back of his neck, avoiding my eyes. "Yeah. I have to admit, I thought the same thing when I heard about that one." There's a long stretch of silence. Just when I think I can't take it any longer, he says. "I have tomorrow off. How about we meet up, discuss what you're thinking. I can't promise anything, but maybe... maybe I can help you find some peace with this, Kate. So you don't run off again."

"Why would that matter?"

His face crumples. His voice is soft, husky as he says, "How could it not? I've missed you. Wakefield feels more like home with you here."

Heat floods into my cheeks and my pulse kicks into overdrive. I bite the inside of my cheek, not sure what to say, afraid it'll be the wrong thing.

"I'm sure your mom and Lily are glad to have you back, too," he adds quickly. "Listen, I've got to get back to work. They just made me the lead on a series of rape cases we discovered are connected. I have to lead the task force meeting in," he looks at his watch and grimaces. "Four minutes. But remember that park down off 14ᵗʰ street that we all used to go to?"

It's a small place only locals know about, hidden from the road and the beach by a grove of sea-grapes. "Yeah."

"Let's meet there. Will noon work for you?"

I nod.

"Great. See you then." He raises a hand at the man who appears in the doorway, tapping at the watch on his wrist. "Gotta go." He stands, seems reluctant to leave. There's something else he wants to say. But he just gives me a tight smile and hurries away.

I watch the door several minutes after he disappears through it. A part of me is disappointed that he didn't want to meet for lunch, or even coffee. But it's not like it's a date. We're meeting to discuss murder. But why did he have to choose somewhere so remote?

TWENTY-FOUR

The restaurant is dim, lit only by the white Christmas lights that zigzag across every inch of the ceiling like stars twinkling in the night sky. It would be incredibly romantic if it weren't for the mariachi band traveling from table to table and the garish decorations covering the walls. A draft from a hidden air duct blows a loose strand of papier-mâché on the pink and white pony piñata hanging over Jeff's head.

But the combination of everything—lighting, music, and décor—meld together to create the perfect, if slightly wacky, atmosphere. I feel more relaxed than I have since I came home. I'm sure the margaritas aren't hurting, either.

"This place is great."

Jeff grins, his eyes twinkling under the strung lights. "I thought you'd like it."

I feel a rush of heat flooding up my neck. Breaking away from his gaze, I take a sip of my drink, trying to remember the things we used to talk about. Not that it will help me make interesting conversation. Jeff's a doctor now. And I... I wait tables. I can't think of a thing to say that could possibly interest him.

I watch as Jeff scoops a chip in salsa, watery red drops raining onto the table on his way to cramming it into his mouth. Maybe he's not so different from the guy I used know after all.

"You'll never guess who I saw today," Jeff says. Squeezing a lime wedge into his beer, he drops it into his glass and says, "Becca."

I smile around my margarita glass.

"I've only run into her a handful of times since I moved back. But now that you're home, it's like the old gang's coming out of the woodwork."

"I saw her, too. I had coffee with her and Mel after Emma's..." The word funeral catches in my chest, down deep, in some dark, hidden cavity.

"Really? How's Mel doing?"

"Same snarky, ice-cold core, just wrapped in a rich outer shell."

Jeff shakes his head, smiling. "So, are you going to get together with them again while you're in town?"

"Why would I do that?"

He straightens up in his seat. "I don't know. You all used to be friends. I just thought that you might."

I shake my head, frowning down at my drink while I stir the ice. I don't know why what he's said has upset me so much. He's just trying to make conversation. But for some reason, I feel myself spiraling down into a funk.

It used to be so easy. So comfortable, like it was earlier today when I was talking to Jimmy. But obviously, things have changed. Now...

The tension grows within the silence between us. The mariachi band reaches our table. I look up, try to force a smile. I can tell by their reactions that it was more of a scowl. They quickly move on to the next table.

Jeff laughs. Reaching across the table, he takes my hand in

his. "Listen, I'm sorry if I upset you. It wasn't my intention. But please, don't bite the entertainment."

My free hand raises to my hair, shielding my face from the restaurant. I can feel my cheeks flaring red. "That *is* what they thought was going to happen, isn't it?" I feel a giggle rising in my chest, a bubble fueled by tequila and lime juice. I'm shaking with pent-up laughter, my eyes watering.

"At least they'll put a rush on our order now."

Squeezing Jeff's fingers, I say, "I'm sorry. I don't know why... I just feel so overwhelmed. It seems like everything's happened so fast. I never even got the chance to... the idea of catching up with Becca and Mel, when I can't with Emma, it just feels wrong."

"I understand."

"You do? Because I don't."

"Maybe you should stop trying, then. You've never been good at dealing when things get tough."

I stick my straw in my mouth and take a long sip of my margarita. He's not wrong. But the truth isn't always an easy thing to hear.

"And grief is messy," he continues. "Sometimes you've just got to go with it, experience it, live through it, and wait until you come out on the other side to see if any sense can be made of it."

"When did you get so wise?"

"My second year of residency."

The server arrives and sets steaming hot plates heaped with food before us. My mouth waters. I focus on the sensation. I can't remember the last time I processed something normal. Something enjoyable.

Maybe Jeff's right. I've been on overload trying to juggle all my conflicting emotions. I can't expect myself not to mourn the loss of my best friend, even if I really lost her years ago.

"You need to be realistic and face the fact that you're not strong enough to handle this on your own."

"What?" I lower the forkful of rice that was almost in my mouth, stunned.

"Don't forget. I know you, Kate. You've always been a wimp about things like this." He holds my gaze over the rim of his cup as he takes a drink. "And I don't want you to run away again. But it's okay. I'm here for you. I'll get you through this."

I sit in numb silence as his words sink in, ashamed that my flaws are so obvious. No wonder no one ever takes me seriously. My face burns up to the tips of my ears with embarrassment.

"Hey, that looks pretty good." He points to the untouched enchilada on my plate. "Can I try it?"

I stare down at the meal that only moments before seemed so tantalizing, finding that I've completely lost my appetite. "Yeah. Sure."

I balance a forkful across the table to his mouth. He takes the bite, his eyes never leaving mine. When he finishes chewing, he gives me the smile that always made my knees go weak. But now it's my whole body that feels frail and feeble.

I don't understand. Jeff wants to help me. It seems like he's willing to take me back, to have everything be just the way it used to be. So then why can I not wait for the night to be over?

TWENTY-FIVE

I must have forgotten to close the blinds last night. I wake up to the blinding sun in my eyes. I turn over, not wanting to let go of the comfort of unconsciousness just yet. But now the band of light streams across the back of my neck and ear. The lit strip of skin heats up, hotter and hotter, until I imagine I can hear my flesh sizzling. With a groan, I give up, shoving the covers down and dragging myself out of bed.

I go through the morning routine my mom and I have established on autopilot, helping her get up, get dressed, get breakfast. I feel a pang of guilt when I park her wheelchair beside Ms. Lynn on the couch, but it's not like their day will be any better if I'm sitting beside them while they watch TV. I'd be nothing but a distraction, anyway. There's no way I could force myself to sit still.

I make a feeble attempt at a couple of chores, sweeping, laundry, but when I go to change the clothes over, I realize that I forgot to turn the washer on, and the floor is still gritty beneath my bare feet. By the time I leave to go meet Jimmy, I'm a jumble of nerves, but I don't know why.

The day is bright, with giant, puffy white clouds gathering in layers overhead. I cruise down A1A, catching glimpses of sparkling turquoise water through people's yards and dune grass. When I reach 14th street, I pull over onto the side of the road, parking the minivan on the grass behind a black Dodge.

I wait several minutes for traffic to break before getting out. Jimmy was right—there does seem to be lots more people here than there used to be. I passed multiple new construction sites on the way here, untamed places where I used to hang out and play as a child now bricked over and landscaped. It makes me feel sad, another thing that I've lost.

I step out into the searing heat and search the sea-grape barricade for the thin yellow trail that leads to the park. As I slip through the opening, vanishing instantly from the road, I wonder if this is such a smart idea. I didn't tell anyone where I was going. No one besides Jimmy knows where I am. Yeah, he's a cop, but I know firsthand that when you look beneath the surface, people aren't always who you think they should be inside.

It's not too late to turn around. Maybe I should call him, tell him I've changed my mind. Or suggest that we meet somewhere else, instead.

A branch cracks ahead and I freeze like a rabbit hoping the coyote won't see it. But predators have a set of skills the rest of us don't. The ability to smell, see, hear things the rest of us can't. Is the scent of my fear noticeable? Can they feel the vibration of my heart?

And then there he is before me, and a tiny voice whispers inside my head, *yes*.

"Hey, Kate, there you are. Sorry, I was heading back out to wait for you so you wouldn't have to walk through here alone. It's kind of gotten a bit more overgrown since the last time I was here. I just wanted to set up, first."

I swallow hard. Set up what? A sudden surge of panic makes me look over my shoulder, wondering how long it would take me to sprint back to the road. But I'm being ridiculous. It's too late to run now. There's no way he wouldn't catch me.

"It's just a few more yards. The gazebo's still there. It's not in the best shape, and it's obviously still used as a party spot." He grimaces as he raises a white trash bag I hadn't noticed in his hand, beer cans and bottles clanging around on the inside. "But it's still... You'll see when you get there. It's like traveling back in time to when things were, I don't know, easy."

Suddenly, I want nothing more than to be in that place. I squeeze past him on the trail, and sure enough, after another ten feet the trail spreads open, revealing a clearing with a gazebo in the middle. It's not at all and yet exactly like I remember.

The gazebo is older, smaller, dingier but yet so obviously still infused with the special magic of youth that I can't help but laugh out loud. It fills me with a brief moment of joy, and as I step closer and see a plastic tablecloth spread over the floor, an assortment of food laid out across it, I'm filled with another.

I turn to Jimmy. "Did you do all this?"

He shrugs, rubbing at the back of his neck. "It's not much. Just figured we might want to eat."

"This is amazing."

"Yeah?" He gives me a shy grin.

"You didn't have to go through so much trouble."

"I wanted to."

"But why? You must be so busy."

"Because I hoped it would make you smile."

I'm shocked by the sweetness of the gesture. I feel my guard lower as we sit there, snacking on pesto pasta salad, curry chicken salad, brie, French bread, and fruit. And it feels so good, to not have my barriers raised for once. Before I know it, I tell Jimmy everything.

About Lily's mutism and the guilt I bear. Emma's collection

of newspaper trophies and how worried I am that she killed other people and that it's my fault for keeping her secret. Mrs. Daley's terminal diagnosis and the niggling awkwardness I still feel wedged between me and my mom. And even though I never thought it would happen, I feel better.

TWENTY-SIX

We sit, staring at each other over half cleared plates and the remains of our picnic. I feel spent, not sure what else to add. I'm afraid I've said too much already.

"So you really think that those newspapers Emma had collected were from murders she committed?" Jimmy asks. He looks pale, his voice tense. With each revelation I divulged, a vein in the center of his forehead became more apparent. I watch it now as it throbs with his pulse, wondering if he regrets meeting me here today, listening to me.

"It makes a sick sort of sense, doesn't it?"

He stares down at the tablecloth, tracing the pattern with a finger. "I don't know. I suppose it does. But..." He holds my gaze for a second, opens his mouth like he's going to speak, then looks away. His lips twist into a knot like he's trying to trap whatever it was he was going to say.

"What?" I ask, brushing a crumb off my lap.

"I just think, maybe, you should keep an open mind. Maybe there was more to what happened that night between Emma and Brad than you saw."

"Like what?"

He shrugs, squints up at the sky, where the sun has made a marked shift to the west. "Maybe it was self-defense."

"You mean?" I can't bring myself to say it. And I can't believe I never thought of it before. I was so quick to jump to the conclusion that my best friend was a cold-blooded killer. But maybe Jimmy's right, and that's not what happened at all.

"Not many people know this, the investigation into Brad's death kind of overshadowed everything else that happened that night. I didn't even find out until years later, after I'd joined the force. But a girl was attacked while we were out there."

I cup a hand to my head as if his words have landed a physical blow. "And you think maybe that's what happened to Emma? Brad attacked her and, what, she fought back and won?"

"I don't know. Maybe. I mean, it's possible. Who knows what happened out there between them? Take these cases I'm working... Whoever this guy is, he's obviously been doing this for a while, but I keep thinking, there were probably other crimes, lesser assaults while he worked his way up to rape. And these women, they fight back, you know. Or, at least, they try. I keep wondering if there were women he attacked who got away."

"But if that's true, then why didn't Emma say anything?" I blink back tears, refusing to let them spill. Jimmy's wrong. He has to be. I couldn't have suspected her all these years if she was innocent. Besides—if what happened with Brad was self-defense, or even an accident, then why did she keep on killing?

"She could have been scared to, worried that she'd be blamed for the crime. Or she could have been in shock. Or maybe she had nothing to do with Brad's death, she was just so stunned when she found him that she picked up the rock. I mean, do we even know for sure that's what killed him?"

"Well, yeah, of course."

"How?"

"It had blood on it."

"There are plenty of ways for blood to get on a rock. Have you ever contacted the Medical Examiner's Office? Looked at the autopsy report?"

"Well, no." This isn't going the way it was supposed to. I already had a surplus of questions without answers. Now I'm starting to doubt what I thought I knew was true. "But what about the other murders?"

"There's no evidence that they're connected."

"But the newspapers..."

"I admit, it's weird. Maybe she felt some kind of a connection to the crimes."

"Okay, but, the timing. How do you explain that all the murders in the newspapers were discovered within days of the anniversary of Brad's death?"

"I don't know what to tell you, Kate. Maybe that date holds significance for someone else. A different killer, a copycat, an accomplice, violent marauders... The thing is, now that Emma's gone, we may never know. I want to help you find the answers you're looking for, and I'm going to do everything within my power to make sure that happens, but I also want to make sure you're going to be okay if it doesn't."

He runs a hand through his hair, leaving it standing on end, and sighs. "If that means playing devil's advocate and telling you things you don't want to hear, well, I'm sorry, but I'm still going to do it. This whole thing has taken enough from us all already. I'm not willing to sacrifice anything else. Especially you."

He's come closer to me while he talks, crawling on his knees until our faces are only a foot apart. He has both of my hands in his, his eyes earnest, beseeching. I can't think straight with him this close to me. I don't want to think at all.

We're frozen in this fragile moment. I imagine hitting the

pause button and staying here forever. Then his phone rings, and the moment shatters.

Jimmy pulls away guiltily, as if surprised to find that the distance between us has vanished. I listen to his side of the conversation, tense, terse, and I know that whatever potential the moment held is gone. He has to go.

Silence stretches between us as I help him pack up. I'm acutely aware of the space between us as he walks me back to the car. And as I sit behind the wheel of my mom's minivan, watching him drive off, I feel the sensation on my lips of some-thing that was never really there.

I feel lost, beyond confused, directionless, unwilling to believe that I could have been wrong about what happened. But now I don't know who—or what—to believe. I need some solid facts, something I can hold on to that I know is true. Somehow, I manage to find my way to the Medical Examiner's Office.

The small, nondescript brick building has few windows, and is the last place I would have expected it, tucked away down a residential street shaded by oaks and surrounded by mobile homes. I feel out of place, like I shouldn't be here, but I'm desperate. All I need is one thing to let me know that I'm on the right track. That I'm not crazy.

As I fill out the request to receive a copy of Brad's autopsy report, I ask for another one of the forms. I'm not sure what it is that I'm doing. Not sure what it is I hope to accomplish. Not sure that I really want to see it.

But still, I hand the completed paperwork over to the recep-tionist, a slightly rounded, grandmotherly type woman with short, salt-and-pepper hair and thick-rimmed glasses, who assures me she'll process my requests and, if they're approved, send a copy of the reports to me in the mail.

Afterwards, sitting in my car in the parking lot, blasting the AC, I watch a pair of little girls playing across the street. They can't be more than five or six, and wear matching hot pink bikinis and swimming floaties on their arms, even though they're only dancing around the kiddie pool centered in the dirt patch of a front yard. They seem so happy and free.

I remember being that way, once. I remember a summer spent splashing in a plastic pool and running through the sprinklers, being a mermaid one minute, a princess the next, giggling and playing in a time before worries and stress and inhibitions. And I remember that it was Emma who was right there beside me, filling my cup with imaginary tea.

I have so many questions, but none of the answers. I feel like I'm on a scavenger hunt without a treasure map. I know the clues exist. Right now, I can think of only one place to find them.

TWENTY-SEVEN

It feels like the night is closing in on them, the trees tightening their embrace, and, for a moment, Kate worries that the woods will never let them leave. That they'll be doomed to wander forever under this darkened sky, an endless loop of terror and guilt as she leads her little sister toward a safety that doesn't exist.

She curses under her breath and continues pulling Lily forward, away from the old orange grove and the body, the sounds of Mel and Becca following not far behind them. Nothing looks familiar, yet everything does. It all looks the same. Have they passed that faded beer can half buried in the sand before, or was that a different one?

And then, she smells it, faint but unmistakable. Smoke. They must be getting close to the clearing, the bonfire, the dunes.

"Kate! Thank God you're alright."

She spins, squints through the inky darkness. "Jimmy?"

"Listen, something's going on. Everyone's taking off. The cops are coming."

As she closes the distance between them, she can see the faint glow of the almost extinguished fire, her former classmates reminding her of seagulls as they group and ungroup, trying to decide what to do. The faint ring of sirens sounds in the distance.

Jimmy gives Lily a sweet smile that goes unreturned. "Everything's going to be okay, kid. Don't worry."

"Where's Jeff?"

"I don't know. He took off a while ago. I thought you were with him. Then I saw your mom's minivan still parked on the street and came back."

She doesn't believe him. Jeff wouldn't have left her behind. He would have made sure she was safe. She doesn't know why, but Jimmy must be lying. And if there's one lesson she's learned tonight about her friends, it's that she can't trust any of them.

TWENTY-EIGHT

The next morning, when Emma's mom answers the door, her face is clouded with confusion. Her features look more sunken, her skull more skeletal. I feel horrible for being here for the wrong reasons.

"Kate, honey, I... I don't think Emma is here right now." She stands back, beckoning me inside.

A sob rises inside me so quickly that it escapes before I can shove it back down. I mask the sound with a cough.

"Oh, dear. I'm sorry, honey. Emma's... well, I suppose she's never coming back. But you know that. Don't worry, I'm not going senile on you. I... I guess it's just one of those things that I want to forget."

I wrap my arms around her. She feels frail in my embrace, her bones brittle. Her heart thumps against my chest with the speed of a hummingbird's wings. The quick fluttering feels like it's covered by only a thin sheet of fabric.

Letting her go, I ask, "How are you doing, Mrs. Daley?"

Her hand flaps dismissively. "That's kind of a loaded question, these days. But I'm glad you're here."

I follow her to the kitchen, take a seat at the table across from her. Stacks of papers cover the top. The edge of a photograph sticks out of one of the piles. An auburn curl, the curve of a cheek, the upturned corner of an almond shaped eye peeks out at me.

Even though I know I shouldn't, I can't help but reach out and push the corner so that more of the picture is revealed. I recognize the photo. On the other side of the frame, my face is pushed up against Emma's. I remember the day it was taken, the happiness I felt, the peace.

"You can have it, if you want."

Looking up, I find Emma's mom staring at me. Studying me.

"Thank you." Sliding the photo from the pile, I set it on the table before me. I'm having trouble not staring at it. At us.

"I want you to take a look around, take anything else you want."

"Oh, no, thank you, but—"

"Whatever you don't take will end up sold or in the trash. Please, Kate. I'd like to know that some of these memories will survive."

Her cloudy eyes water. Thin lips tremble in a wavering line. My eyes ask the question I can't speak.

"I'm going into a hospice. Can't take it all with me." She shrugs, smiling weakly. Her tone is light, but I see the heartbreak etched across her expression.

"Of course. Thank you, I'd be honored."

"Take your time looking, take whatever you want. I'm sure there are some things in Emma's room that you'd like. You'll have to send Lily over, too, but you should have first pick. I'd like to leave you girls the house, but... I don't know, yet. They might have to sell it to cover my stay. I guess it depends on how long it is."

Tears slice down my cheeks, carved deep by a knife of grief, hot like blooddrops as they trickle off my chin into my lap.

Emma's mom reaches across the table, slides a stack of papers out of the way to take my hand. She squeezes.

"Don't cry for me. It's a good thing. Really. I've stayed here far too long already."

I wonder where she means by here. This house? This life?

"Anyway, it'll be nice not having to fix my own meals anymore. And when the time comes, well, it'll be nice not to be alone."

I nod, forcing a smile, because, really, it's ridiculous that she's the one comforting me right now. "When?"

"Three days. Four. I've got a couple of loose ends I need to wrap up first. I need to find the deed to the house, mainly. And like I said, I'd like for you and Lily to give some of these things a home."

"If there's anything I can do?"

"There is. First, find what you want to keep. That's what I want the most. Then you can help me if I still haven't found that damn deed. I swear, it's got to be in one of these stacks, somewhere. I've looked at almost every piece of paper in the house already. Now get."

She shoos me away with her hand. Standing, I slowly make my way out of the kitchen into the hall. I lean against the wall a minute, finding my bearings. My eyes focus on the door at the far end. Behind it is Emma's room.

It seems odd, having permission to rifle through her things, to take whatever I'd like, but maybe it's also a sign. An omen that I'm on the right path, that everything will fall in line and make sense if I just try.

My legs are unsteady, my gait jerky as I near the door. I feel like music should be playing, some creepy score from a scary movie, building suspense. I know I'm being silly and overdramatic, like I'm expecting something sinister to jump out at me and give me a big scare, but I can't help it. I kind of hope that something like that does happen. That it will be that easy.

I tell myself it's like a Band-Aid, you just have to rip it off quickly and get it over with. One, two, three, and it's done. But sometimes the sting that follows is worse than if you had slowed down and taken your time.

I push the door open. It's the same room where I've spent countless nights sleeping, unknown hours primping and preparing, so much time just being. The décor is nicer now.

A reclaimed barnwood dresser and armoire have replaced the white wicker Emma had growing up. The endless collage of band posters has been replaced by a few nice prints, scenes of cerulean waves rolling up onto empty shores at either sunrise or sunset. There's still a clutter of accessories on every surface, and I know that if I open the closet door, an avalanche of shoes will chase me, but the room of adult Emma has a much different feel than it used to. Much calmer and more subdued.

It gives me my first clue about the person Emma had become. Opening the top drawer of the dresser, I look inside. Socks in neat rows on one side, undergarments on the other. Tidily stacked T-shirts in the next drawer, followed by a drawer of shorts, and another of pants.

It's all so neat. Emma's drawers used to be a wild jumble of whatever she could shove into them with no regard for order. I guess it makes sense that she would have become more organized, especially if she went so long as a serial killer without getting caught.

The thought sneaks up on me, striking with such force that the air is knocked from my lungs. Staggering back, I take a seat on the bed, my head spinning. I need a moment to sit, think, acknowledge my feelings. But I have to move on.

Pulling open the nightstand, I rifle through the contents. Lotion, a handful of lip balms, a small plastic photo album, and half of a heart shaped necklace. I take the last two items out. Holding the necklace in my palm, I run my fingers over the inscribed surface, then slip it into my pocket. I have its other half. It's one of the few things I took with me when I left. It's never left my possession.

Flipping through the album, I see it's filled with pictures from senior year. My face, Emma's, Becca's, Melinda's, even Lily's face flash by. I place it in the center of the bed, starting a pile of things to take with me. In the closet, I find a box of mementos; concert tickets, movie stubs, select notes that we wrote to each other during class over the years. I add it to my stack, wanting to look through it later.

I decide to take her letter jacket from volleyball, a shoebox of photos, and a pen holder she made freshmen year in pottery class. As an afterthought, I add the prints from her wall. They were what she chose to look at every day. Knowing that somehow makes me feel closer to her, which I need right now if I'm going to figure this out, because I'm not finding anything that sheds any insight into what was going on with Emma.

I leave the room much the way I found it. Carrying my armload of treasures into the kitchen, I find Emma's mom looking as victorious as I imagine a dying woman can look.

"Found it," she says, waving a handful of papers in the air. "And it looks like you found a few things, too. Good. I knew you would." She smiles with the first real happiness I've seen since my return. "There are a few other things I want you to take." She gestures to the counter, where a reusable cloth grocery bag sits full of photo albums, leaning on top of a purse. "Along with any of the furniture you want."

A knock on the door startles us both. She looks over her shoulder, at the digital clock on the stove. "Shoot. It's the nurse. I was hoping we'd have more time." Struggling to her feet, she points at the pile on the counter until I grab the shopping bag, slipping the handles up onto my shoulder. "The purse, too."

I look at her, my forehead furrowed so low that I can see part of my eyebrows in the upper range of my vision.

"It was Emma's favorite," she explains. "The police returned it to me. I'd like for you to have it."

Reluctantly, I slide my arm through the loop, letting the bag hang from the crook of my elbow, as I follow her to the door.

"Rose Marie, welcome, come on inside."

"You're looking well today, Debbie."

"I am, aren't I?" Emma's mom asks.

The nurse named Rose Marie gives me a nod, a curious expression pinching the edges of her face. I consider introducing myself, but Emma's mom puts a quick end to the awkwardness hanging in the air between us.

"You go on into the kitchen, I'll be there in just a sec."

She watches Rose Marie's retreating form, then turns to me, reaching her arm around my shoulders. "You come back tomorrow, okay, sweetie. There are some more things for you to take." She looks up at me, eyes shining, a soft bloom of color tinting her wrinkled linen cheeks.

"I love you girls so much. You and your sisters. All three of you are such good girls." Standing on tiptoe, she presses her dry lips to my cheek, then pushes me out the door and closes it behind me.

I walk to the minivan in a daze. Dumping my load of goods into the back, I glance at the front door again, eyes squinted against more than just the sun. Sisters? I climb behind the wheel and start the car, adjusting the AC vent as I stare at the door again. Shaking my head, I put the car in reverse and back down the drive, determined to forget, but the word keeps echoing in my mind. Sisters.

TWENTY-NINE

I'm back home in time for lunch. I roll my mom's wheelchair up to the table, then watch as she and Ms. Lynn take their first few bites of the sandwiches I've brought. When I'm satisfied that they like them, I sit down and join in.

"These are good, Kate. Thank you."

I beam a thousand-watt smile at my mom. It's been such a long, full day already, but instead of being worn out, I feel energized. And grateful. Very, very grateful that besides her broken hip, which is mending, my mom is in good health. A small part of me is relieved that this all happened now, that I was forced to come home while there's still time for us to spend together, to repair the bridge that spans the distance between us.

"They are," Ms. Lynn says. "Did you get them at that little deli on the corner of Azalea and Hibiscus?"

I nod, chewing.

"You know what other place those people own?" No one asks but Ms. Lynn answers anyways. "That little hippie store that's beachside. Something Dreams. You know which one, Maureen, the one that Emma worked at."

"Emma worked at a hippie store?"

The words pop out of my mouth with a puff of disbelief and a few breadcrumbs.

"Mm-hmm. I believe they refer to it as a 'Holistic Gift Store', but still. Such a shame. You girls, all of you, so smart, but no ambition. Now, back in my day, being a woman, you really had to fight if you wanted to get an education and do something with your life."

"Oh, hush, Marilla. You're not *that* old." My mom rolls her eyes at me.

Ms. Lynn ignores her. "Now me, I wasn't smart, so I had to work and fight even harder, and I managed to make something of myself. And I guarantee you your mother was one of the only women in class when she went to law school. But you girls, you are all so smart, and not a one of you went to college to get your education. Instead, you girls wait tables and cashier like it's the 1950s and you don't have any choice."

"Marilla."

"No, Maureen, she needs to hear this. Her and her sister, who, Lord knows, has never even had a job. The girl can't even drive, for God's sake! I don't know why you allow that child to stay so sheltered. It isn't healthy."

"Marilla!"

I'm surprised at the sternness in my mother's voice. Ms. Lynn must be, too, because she gives my mom the side-eye and moves on.

"Anyways, Kate, it's not too late. I read an article about a woman in her seventies who just graduated college. If she can do it, you can. And I want you to know that if you do decide to give it a try, I'd be more than happy to help with your tuition."

Shock rolls over me in waves. Doubt, amazement, gratitude, all crash against the shore of my consciousness. Overwhelmed, I get up and wrap my arms around Ms. Lynn, her fuzzy gray hair tickling my cheek.

"Now don't go getting all soggy on me, hun," she says,

giving my arm a squeeze and a pat. "Sit down and finish your lunch. I said I'd help, not give you a free ride."

I kiss her powdery cheek and return to my seat. "That's very generous of you, Ms. Lynn. Thank you for the offer."

"Well, are you going to accept it, or not?"

She and my mom are firing looks across the table at each other, an entire operatic saga without words. I have a feeling this is something they've discussed before.

"I..." I want nothing more than to say yes. Skipping college is just one of my umpteen regrets. It's also one of the few that can still be righted. "I'm going to need some time to think about it. But I'm considering it. Seriously."

Ms. Lynn nods, examining her sandwich. "Good girl," she says, then takes a bite. She doesn't look at me, but her head bobs softly as she chews.

We finish our lunch in silence. When they're done, I settle my mom back next to the couch for another round of TV with Ms. Lynn. I feel guilty leaving her so much, not finding something better to occupy her time with, but it's not like we can go take a walk on the beach.

But maybe, if everything works out, I'll stick around, take Ms. Lynn up on her offer. The past couple of weeks have shown me what I've been missing. That the place I feared so much isn't so bad at all.

Suddenly, there's nothing more that I want in the world than for Wakefield to be home again. To return to the place of my family, my friends, my memories. But for that to happen, I need to take this place back. I need to tear it away from the grasp of that night, sweep away the cobwebs and shadows, make it clean and whole again. For that, I need answers. And now I know one more place where I might get some.

THIRTY

Piscean Dreams is one of those new-age stores that smells like incense and has employees in tie-dye and dreadlocks. The floors are covered in handwoven mats, and crazy, indie artwork covers every inch of wall not blocked by displays. I have a feeling I'm the only thing containing gluten in the store.

The parking lot was empty. The bike rack was full. A girl wearing a name tag with April written in curvy, rainbow letters, who I vaguely recognize, sits on a stool behind the register up front, reading a book. I expect it to be some groovy self-help or how to be a witch manual, but as I get closer, I see that it's the latest Jodi Picoult. Marking her place, she sets the book down and greets me with a friendly smile.

I have absolutely no idea where to begin, so I just go for it. "Hi, I was hoping to talk with someone about my friend who used to work here. Emma Daley."

She scratches at the traces of henna artwork stenciled onto the back of her hand. Sniffing thickly, her eyes turn damp and pink. "I knew Emma. You're Kate, right?"

"Yeah."

"We went to school together. I was a few years behind you."

"I thought you looked familiar."

"Emma and I were friends. I mean, as much as she was friends with anyone. She didn't really go out, she wasn't much into the social scene, but we hung together a bit. What is it that you want to know?"

"What can you tell me?"

Her face creases in a frown.

"Sorry, that's kind of broad, isn't it? It's just, Emma and I, we were best friends growing up. But we fell out of touch, and I'm having trouble understanding some of what was going on with her. I thought that maybe if I talked with someone who knew her more recently, that maybe I'd get a sense of how she might have changed."

April's eyes do a circuit of the ceiling while she considers what I've said. Finally, she looks at me, the smile back on lips that are stained deep purple. "That makes sense, I guess. Emma was, I don't know, special. But I guess I don't have to tell you that. She was the sweetest person I've ever met. Always bending over backward to help, never asking for anything in return. You could always count on her if you needed someone to pick up a shift for you. I mean, she'd work herself to the bone. There were days where she could barely use her hands by the end of the day, but she just kept smiling. At least, until her mom got sick."

"She changed then?"

"I wouldn't say changed. Maybe just became, I don't know, preoccupied, I guess. Kind of tired and run-down. But, I mean, you could understand why she wanted to spend more time at home and less at work."

"Was she really upset about her mom?"

"At first, yeah. She was stunned. But then she seemed to come to terms with it. Found some peace. She developed a really positive attitude about her mom's prognosis."

"She thought she was going to recover?"

"Well, not exactly. But she had just found this clinical trial for a new palliative chemo that she was super excited about. Something that was really having great results at extending the life and comfort of terminal patients. She came in right after she had talked to one of the research assistants about getting her mom in on the study, and it sounded hopeful. Emma was over the moon."

"When was this?"

"Just a few days before she, you know."

It feels like she just pushed the plunger on a syringe of ice, a shot of freezing slush flooding my veins.

"Do you know if anything changed? With the research trial?"

"Not that I know of, no. I swapped shifts with her so she could take her mom to some clinic in Orlando that Friday to make sure she qualified for the study. But I guess that never happened, huh?"

I'm only half listening to what she says as the synapsis in my brain fire away, making connections.

"Is there anything else that you can think of?"

"Not really. Oh, except we still have one of her EpiPens in the fridge in the break room. I know those things are kind of expensive, didn't know if her mom might be able to use it and want it back?"

"I don't think so. Her mom doesn't have an allergy like she did. Maybe you'll have a customer who needs it someday." The idea seems simpler than explaining that Emma's mom is entering hospice.

"Yeah, maybe."

"Thank you, April. You've been a lot of help."

"No problem."

I force a smile and turn to leave, stumbling off a display of healing crystals. I catch my balance before I knock anything over and head for the door, dazed.

"Oh, hey, Kate?"

I freeze, not knowing what to expect when I turn around. April looks at me with a sympathetic smile, eyes soft.

"Emma still considered you her best friend, you know. I don't know what happened between you two. I asked, once, but all she said was that you guys would work it out eventually, because best friends always do. I just thought you should know that."

I blink at the tears threatening to invade my eyes. My nose burns. My throat is tight. When I speak, I have to push the words past the lump lodged in their way. "Thank you, April. Really."

I manage to make it to the parking lot before the tears attack like a horde of Vikings. I sit on the curb, hugging my knees to my chest. Emma had more faith in me than I had in myself. She was a good, sweet person. She was a cold-blooded killer. Some of these thoughts make sense. Others don't.

Right now, what stands out most of all, is why would Emma kill herself the day before she planned to take her mom for screening to join a research trial that could prolong her life? The answer is that she wouldn't. So then, what happened? Was Emma's death really just an accident?

Did she have so much going on with juggling all her murders and trying not to get caught that she started unraveling, forgetting the EpiPen that she'd kept on her at all times for decades? Or was there something else at play, something I haven't thought of yet? I roughly rub my tears away with my fists, gritting my teeth in frustration. Once again, I've hit a wall, finding only questions and no answers.

THIRTY-ONE

The house is so quiet that the sound of the empty air is deafening. My mom went to bed hours ago. I have no idea whether Lily is home or not. I try sleeping. I try watching a movie to distract myself. I try reading a book. But nothing can keep me out of my own mind, and I'm driving myself insane.

I need to talk to someone. In the old days, if Emma wasn't available, I'd talk to Jeff, but I don't feel comfortable talking to him about this. About her. Especially considering they have some kind of history together, without me.

I consider calling one of my old roommates from Boston. Someone with no emotional attachment to the situation, who could give me a detached point of view, but after the text she sent when she found out I'd taken off without saying anything, I have a feeling that the call wouldn't go as well as I would hope.

I even think about calling Becca. I find the crumpled receipt with her number in my purse, lay it out on the dresser, pick up my phone. But I just can't bring Becca in on this, I'm not sure why. Maybe it would make it too real.

Oddly, what I want most is to call Jimmy. Even though he was Jeff's best friend in high school, we never really spent much time together. But now... I crave the soothing tone of his voice, the calming safety of his company. And that makes me feel awkward as hell.

So, it's just me and my runaway imagination, pacing across the tiny bedroom floor, trying to tire myself out and calm down and kill time until I can go see Emma's mom again in the morning. It's not working. It's like a horde of bees are swarming beneath the surface of my skin, making it impossible to hold still.

My eyes fall on Emma's purse. It sits on top of the mound of stuff I brought home and dumped in the corner of my room earlier today. My hand strikes out like a snake, snatching it from the pile and dumping the contents out on the bed before I have the chance to think twice. I shuffle through the jumble on the duvet. Comb, Kleenex, lip balm, wallet, keys, balled-up scraps of paper, a lone breath mint with a piece of lint stuck to it, and a wine cork.

A wine cork. Picking it up for closer inspection, I turn it over in my hand, knowing what I'll find. I run my thumb over the flakey nub surrounding the puncture mark.

They said that Emma hadn't been carrying an EpiPen on her when she had her reaction. But maybe they were wrong. Just because it wasn't on Emma when they found her doesn't mean she hadn't been carrying one. Maybe whoever had collected her effects didn't know what they were looking at.

They couldn't have known that when Emma had a reaction, sometimes even just to peanut dust in the air, that her hands swelled. That her fingers got numb and puffy and lost their dexterity so quickly that Emma couldn't remove the cap off the needle. That Emma was accustomed to removing the caps and replacing them with wine corks, so the needle was protected, but if she needed to use it by herself, she could, grabbing the wine cork between her teeth and pulling the needle out.

Maybe the authorities investigating her death wouldn't have

known that, but there are others who should have told the police what to look for. Like Jeff, for starters. He said he was there at the hospital when they brought her in. Wouldn't he, especially as a doctor, have said something?

And Jimmy. I watch TV, I know the police would have made an itemized list of the contents of Emma's handbag. Why did they think she carried a wine cork in her purse? Could so many people really have accidentally overlooked such an important detail?

I can understand why Mrs. Daley might not have noticed. Unless she did. Is this the reason why she wanted me to have the purse—so I'd know that Emma *did* have her EpiPen on her that day, that it had somehow, mysteriously, gone missing? Or was it taken?

But that doesn't make sense. There's no reason for someone to take Emma's emergency epinephrine unless they planned to... I drop the wine cork like it's a hot coal, staring at it in horror as it bounces across the carpet. Because the only reason someone would take Emma's EpiPen was if they wanted to let her die. Or worse, possibly even kill her.

Is it possible that Emma was murdered?

A shiver courses through my body, staying in my jaw as a light tremor. Someone out there must know more about this than they're letting on. And if that's true, then they have a reason for keeping the secret. Possibly a killer reason. Chances are, I know who it is. The only question is, how closely do I know them?